Also by Angela Cervantes:

Gaby, Lost and Found
Allie, First at Last
Me, Frida, and the Secret of the Peacock Ring

LETY OUT LOUD

BY
ANGELA CERVANTES

SCHOLASTIC INC.

ISBN 978-1-338-15935-6

10 9 8 7 6 5 4 3   20 21 22 23 24

Printed in the U.S.A.   40
This edition first printing 2020

Book design by Nina Goffi

This title won the 2020
Pura Belpré Honor Award Medal
for the U.S. edition published by
Scholastic Inc. in 2019.

TO MY HUMAN SIBLINGS: LORENZO, RIO, ENRIQUE,
AND
MY FURRY, FOUR-LEGGED SIBLINGS: CHEECH AND CHONG

CHAPTER 1

Furry Friends Summer Camp

If Lety Muñoz could adopt any animal in the world, it would be Spike, the sweet black-and-white terrier sitting across from her on the lawn at that very minute. Lety was outside the Furry Friends Animal Shelter along with other summer campers. All of them wore shorts and teal-blue Furry Friends T-shirts and sat quietly as the shelter's owner and veterinarian, Dr. Villalobos, told stories about the various dogs and cats at the shelter. Lety liked how Dr. Villalobos's voice rose high with excitement and then dropped low when a story turned serious. He had colorful tattoos on both arms and long, dark hair pulled into a braid that snaked down his back. He was like no other veterinarian Lety had ever seen. Still, it was Spike that drew her gaze. The small dog wore a blue bandanna and gnawed at a twisted piece of rope.

"Our shelter is full of dogs and cats that were surrendered by their families," Dr. Villalobos said. "Others were picked up as strays by our rescue team. Spike was brought to the shelter for the first time by highway patrol. He was chasing cars. Can you believe it?"

Giggles and gasps erupted from the campers, but Lety was stuck on Dr. Villalobos's words: "brought to the shelter for the first time." She wanted to raise her hand and ask what he meant. Had there been a second and third time? Luckily, Dr. Villalobos began to explain.

"Spike doesn't have a winning record with forever families," he said. "He knows how to high-five, shake hands, and roll over, and thanks to one of our volunteers, he's finally mastered how to sit and stay, but every time he's adopted, he's brought back to the shelter. Everyone says he's too wild."

Spike let out a playful bark, as if saying, "That's right!"

Lety shook her head in disbelief. Too wild? She'd only just met Spike, but to her Spike seemed like the perfect dog. He was super cute with his glossy black-and-white coat, pearly white teeth, and warm brown eyes. He was smart, too, and barked every time Dr. V. mentioned him. What kind of people would give him up?

"The good news is that Spike is going home with a foster family today."

One of the kids started to clap and soon all the kids joined in, but Lety hesitated. In just the few minutes she'd been at the shelter, she had already fallen in love and wanted Spike for herself. She didn't want to clap for him leaving. Lety nudged her best friend, Kennedy McHugh, who was sitting next to her.

"What is a foster family?" Lety whispered. "Can someone still adopt Spike?"

"Let me ask," Kennedy said, raising her hand. Lety smiled, relieved that Kennedy was always willing to speak up for her when she wasn't sure the correct way to ask something or didn't want to sound stupid in front of other kids. Dr. Villalobos called on her right away.

"Will Spike still be available for adoption?"

"Yes, but I'm putting him on hold for now," he answered. "Some time with a foster family is the best thing for Spike.

He's become super popular after being on the news this past weekend. And now the whole city wants to adopt him," Dr. Villalobos continued. "Does anyone know what he did?"

"I think I saw it on the news," one of the campers shouted. Lety hadn't seen anything on the news. At home, her parents watched only a Spanish news station, and it covered everything going on in Mexico and Central America, but nothing about Kansas City.

"If you saw it on TV, then you know that Spike is a star now," Dr. Villalobos continued. Lety leaned forward as Dr. V. explained that last Friday one of the shelter volunteers took Spike for a walk to improve Spike's leash walking.

"Taking a leisurely stroll on a leash is a serious accomplishment for Spike," Dr. Villalobos said. "Spike has only two speeds: roadrunner and rocket blaster."

All of the kids chuckled, except Lety. Again, she nudged Kennedy.

"What is a 'rocket blaster'?"

"He means a spaceship sort of thing," Kennedy answered.

"Rocket blaster." Lety repeated the words to herself. She imagined Spike in a space suit blasting off into the sky over the clouds, wagging his tail as he zoomed into space. She laughed.

"Spike was strolling along on his leash when, without warning, he pulled free from the volunteer," Dr. V. said. "With the leash dangling behind him like an extra tail, he darted off toward a parking lot. When the volunteer finally caught up to him, she found Spike scratching and whining at a car. This was strange behavior, even for him. So the volunteer looked inside the car and quickly saw why Spike was upset."

Dr. V. paused. All the kids wriggled with anticipation. Lety bit down on her lower lip, wondering what was inside the car: A fresh pile of dog bones? A long-lost dog sibling whose scent Spike had never forgotten?

"In the backseat, with all the windows closed, was a crying baby girl. This was Friday afternoon. Do you remember how hot it was on Friday?"

Lety gasped. Since school had let out two weeks ago, she and Kennedy had spent almost every day at Kennedy's neighborhood pool. It was so hot last Friday that Lety's watermelon Popsicle melted into a pink sticky puddle before she had a chance to have a taste. While they swam, the radio DJ kept warning everyone that they were under an "orange ozone alert" and to drink lots of water.

"I'd like to leave her parents in a hot car," grumbled Hunter Farmer from under a baseball cap.

Lety knew Hunter from school. He had also been a fifth grader last year at El Camino Charter Elementary, but he was in Mrs. Morgan's class and not Mrs. Camacho's. Mrs. Camacho had all the English Language Learners like Lety as well as other students like Kennedy. She called the English Language Learners her "ELLs," which made Lety think of slimy sea creatures. She didn't want to be an ELL, she wanted to be just another El Camino student who could say things like "my bad" and "cool" and have a smart dog like Spike.

"Was the baby okay?" Kennedy asked.

"The volunteer called 911 and the child was saved," said Dr. Villalobos. "Now everyone wants to adopt the hero dog that saved a child." Dr. V. leaned down and gave Spike a big smooch on his head. The terrier turned away from his rope long enough to swipe Dr. V. with two wild licks. Dr. V. wiped his face with the sleeve of his *Star Wars* T-shirt. What a dog, Lety thought.

"Spike will be going home to a close family friend of mine today where he can run around, chase squirrels, growl at his own shadow, and all the other crazy things he does. And the moral of this story is what? Anyone want to take a stab at what you learned from this amazing dog?"

All of the kids raised their hands, but Lety hesitated.

She had to collect the words just right in her head before she spoke them. As Dr. V. began calling on the other campers, she hoped no one took her answer before she could put the words together.

"Do not forget your babies in the car," said Brisa Quispe with a snap of her fingers that made all the kids laugh and add their own snaps. Lety looked over at Brisa and flashed her a thumbs-up for the sassy answer. Never boring, Brisa responded with a formal salute that made Lety giggle.

Besides Kennedy, Brisa was also one of Lety's best friends. She'd been her best friend since they met in fourth grade when Brisa arrived from La Paz, Bolivia. Lety, who had arrived in the United States from Mexico the year before, was assigned to be Brisa's desk buddy. As her desk buddy, she helped Brisa understand assignments and how things worked in the classroom. Together, Lety and Brisa charged through English spelling words, verbs, and contractions. In no time at all, Brisa and Lety weren't just desk buddies. They were lunchroom buddies, recess buddies, sleepover buddies, and summer pool-time buddies.

"Good answer. Anyone else take away a lesson?" Dr. V. asked.

"Listen to your dog," Kennedy said.

"Good. Next?"

"People are stupid and dogs are smart," Hunter said.

"A little harsh." Dr. Villalobos winked at Hunter. "But in this case, you're mostly right. Anyone else?"

Lety raised her hand and Dr. V. called on her.

"Sometimes people or pets that are unwanted can still become heroes if we just give them a chance," Lety offered.

Dr. Villalobos nodded and slapped his hands together.

"Best answer of the day." He beamed. "Brilliant!"

Lety tried to suppress a smile, but holding back a smile was like trying to keep Spike from being a rocket blaster. She let the smile pour over her entire face, proud that she had taken her time to find the correct words. It was something she had been working on for the past year with Mrs. Camacho's encouragement. Then, as if Spike also understood how important speaking up was to her, he dropped the rope he'd been chewing, trotted over, and gave her a few licks on her cheek. She buried her face in his fur and gave the hero dog a hug while Kennedy and Brisa nuzzled in to give Spike a few loving pets, too. Above all the coos and baby talk from Kennedy and Brisa, Lety heard Hunter's voice.

"More like dumbest answer of the day."

ChapteR 2

Sorry, Not Sorry

Lety was still thinking about what Hunter had said as she followed shelter volunteer Alma Gomez and the rest of the campers on a tour. Lety wasn't sure what she'd done or said to make him act so rude toward her.

As Alma led the campers into a large room stacked with bags of dry pet food, Lety glanced at Hunter. He dragged behind everyone with his hands dug deep into his jean pockets and grimaced under his baseball cap at the pungent fishy-beefy pet food smell that filled the room. Some of the kids pinched their noses to seal out the heavy stench, but Lety didn't think it was so bad. She'd smelled worse back home when she lived in Tlaquepaque, Mexico. On the street where she lived, the sewers backed up after every heavy rain, filling her street with a stink that was a mix of rotten meat and dirty-soggy rags. This smell is nothing! Lety thought to herself.

As if Alma had read Lety's mind, she noticed the campers' reactions and rolled her eyes.

"Forget the smells. Focus on the feels," Alma said.

"Focus on the feels!" Brisa sang. "I like this *chica*, don't you?"

Lety nodded. She did like Alma. Alma had just finished sixth grade at St. Ann's. She had long, dark curly hair pulled back from her face by a purple headband that matched her purple volunteer T-shirt. She told the campers that she had started volunteering at Furry Friends Animal Shelter with her sixth-grade class this past school year. She loved it so much that she wanted to continue through the summer. Because of that, Alma knew all the staff and animals at the shelter. Lety liked how Alma talked about all the pets as if they were family and how throughout the tour, whenever staff saw her coming, they called her name with a smile. "Let's stop here and I'll introduce you to our pantry supervisor and another volunteer," Alma said. She waved at two men hauling large bags of dog food. The two men smiled wide when they saw Alma and quickly put the bags down. When they approached, they each gave Alma a fist bump.

"These are our summer heroes for the next four weeks," Alma explained to the men. "They represent four different schools, including my school, St. Ann's." Alma put an arm around a girl named Lily, who Lety had met when she arrived that morning. The girl flashed a peace sign at them.

"They'll be here for two hours, four days a week, learning about animals, doing crafts, and helping us with some special projects that Dr. Villalobos put together."

"Special projects?" one of the men said. He arched his eyebrows. "Any of them involve helping us here in the pantry? We could use extra help with the pet food bags."

"We may have a few brave ones who won't be offended by the lovely aroma of beef kibble," Alma said. "I'll send them your way!"

The last stop of the tour was to the Bow Wow Zone, where Alma explained they kept the large dogs. All of the kids clapped and howled in excitement to see the dogs, but Lety noticed that Hunter's face remained soured.

"What's Hunter's problem? He doesn't like dogs?" Lety whispered to Brisa and Kennedy, gesturing toward Hunter.

"I think that's just his face," Kennedy said. "It always looks like that."

"He has the face of a llama right before it is about to spit," Brisa said. "Be careful."

Kennedy laughed out loud like it was the funniest thing she'd heard, but Lety couldn't stop worrying about what she'd ever done to Hunter to deserve his mean comment. The whole time she'd been at El Camino Charter, they'd never even talked. They didn't hang out with the same group of friends. Lety's friends mostly consisted of other English Language Learners like Aziza from Uzbekistan, Gazi from Albania, Myra from Puerto Rico, Santiago from El Salvador, and Brisa. The kids hardly ever mixed with the other students. It was something that secretly bothered Lety. No matter how much they improved in English, their other classmates still treated them like they were from another planet. They were never invited to birthday parties. They didn't share their lunch table. When they had to play team sports, the ELLs got selected last unless it was soccer. If it was soccer, Santiago, Brisa, and Gazi were always selected in the top five.

That's why one day when Irish-American Dance Club president Kennedy McHugh stopped Lety in the hallway and asked her about *cascarones*, Lety stood shocked and didn't answer right away.

"Do you know how to make *cascarones*?" Kennedy asked again. Lety gave her a blank stare. Kennedy took Lety's silence as a sign that she wasn't pronouncing the word correctly. "Hold on. Give me one sec . . . it's in this book." Kennedy opened up a paperback book and flipped through a few pages. "The girl in this book makes *cascarones* for Easter. It sounds really fun. They bust them on people's heads." She giggled and stopped on a page. "See, this word here." She pointed out the italicized word *cascarones* to Lety.

"I know how to make them," Lety said.

"Can you teach me? I want to bust them on people's heads."

"What people?" Lety asked.

"Mostly boys. Especially my big brothers."

From that point on, Kennedy and Lety were bona fide best friends. It was Kennedy who had convinced both Lety and Brisa to sign up for the animal shelter summer camp. It was open only to students who had completed fifth grade. This summer, she said, would be their only chance. Lety had spent every summer since arriving in the United States in summer school improving her English, but Kennedy had begged her to try something different. Lety, eager to break away from being called an ELL, jumped at the chance. Brisa was unconvinced that walking dogs and feeding kittens would improve her English, but she wanted to be wherever Lety went, so she signed up, too.

Inside the Bow Wow Zone, Alma led the campers past several cages filled with a mix of German shepherds, Labradors, American pit bulls, and hounds, as well as other mixed breeds that Lety didn't recognize. Alma stopped in front of the cage where a brown-and-black Labrador/shepherd named Finn rested. As they gathered around Finn's cage, the dog shot up from his bed and started barking.

"Who's wearing a hat?" Alma asked, scanning the group of campers. Everyone looked around, confused. What was the big deal with wearing a hat? Lety pointed at Hunter.

"Hey, you in the hat. Come up front," Alma said. Hunter moved up to where Alma stood. "What's your name?"

"Hunter Farmer," he answered. A few of the kids chuckled.

Alma's eyebrows raised in surprise. "So which is it? Are you a hunter or farmer?"

More kids laughed. Hunter shifted uncomfortably. Lety couldn't help but laugh out loud, and Hunter gave her a quick side glare. Brisa nudged her.

"*Cuidado*, the llama is going to spit," she whispered.

"Neither," Hunter answered, shrugging. Alma winked at him.

"I'm dying to know your middle name," she said.

"It's Aaron."

"Okay, Hunter Aaron Farmer," said Alma with a satisfied grin. "Do you want Finn to stop barking?"

"I guess." Hunter shrugged again.

"Then do me a favor — please take off your hat," Alma said. Hunter stepped back, unsure. "Trust me. You'll see what happens."

Hunter reached for his baseball cap and pulled it off. As soon as the hat was off his head of brownish-blond hair, Finn stopped barking and trudged back to his bed. All the kids gasped. Hunter gave Alma an are-you-for-real look.

"Okay, put your hat back on," Alma instructed.

Hunter did as she asked. Finn immediately jumped up and started barking again.

"He really hates hats!" Brisa squealed over Finn's barking. All the kids laughed and excitedly yelled at Hunter to take it off again. Hunter did, and then kept it folded in his hand.

Once Finn quieted and went back to his blue blanket, Alma continued.

"This is Finn. He was surrendered by his family because they had some sort of medical emergency and could no longer take care of him. He's five years old, almost sixty pounds, and he goes berserk when people wear hats around him."

"Why hats?" Hunter asked.

"No idea. Dr. Villalobos talked to his former family and they didn't know. It just started once he arrived here," Alma explained. "But check it out: The reason I'm bringing you to meet the big dogs is because as you can see, we are jam-packed. As part of the summer camp, you'll be learning about what we do, but also helping us with different projects to help all of our furry friends. I've written up all of the projects in the multipurpose room, which will be our home base for the summer camp. Follow me."

Inside the multipurpose room, a group of volunteers stood around in front of large sheets of white paper taped to the walls. The volunteers all wore the same purple volunteer T-shirt as Alma. As they introduced themselves, some explained they were retired grandparents, while others were college students home for the summer. One at a time, each volunteer explained the different projects and tried to convince the campers to pick their project by saying what was so much fun about it. Lety scanned each project: Cat Hero and Dog Hero, Social Media Hero, Food Pantry Hero, and

Shelter Scribe. Kennedy and Brisa were excited to serve as cat heroes, but Lety remained unsure until Alma described the role of the shelter scribe.

"We need someone to write ten animal profiles," Alma said. "These profiles provide visitors a glimpse into the animal's life. Where they come from, their favorite activities . . . stuff like that. We really need someone who likes to write because our shelter scribe, my best friend, Gaby, is gone for the summer."

"Is she the one who wrote these profiles?" Kennedy asked, pointing to the bulletin board, where three profiles were pinned up. The profiles were for Coco, a brown-and-white cat surrendered to the shelter by her family; Milagro, a black kitten dumped into the wild with his siblings; and Kiwi, a light gray kitten.

"Yes, she wrote all of those as part of our school community project this past school year. So while she's away, we need at least one person to take this over."

"Do it!" Brisa whispered into Lety's ear.

"You do it," Lety said, handing Brisa a red marker.

"No way. You write English better than me," Brisa said, nodding and shoving the red marker back at Lety. Lety took the marker, knowing that what Brisa said was true. Lety was a better writer in English than Brisa, because she'd had more years with ELL classes, but Brisa could write really well in Spanish.

When Brisa wrote emails to her family back home in Bolivia, Lety envied Brisa's Spanish writing skills. Before coming to the USA, Brisa attended a private Jesuit school in Bolivia. She learned to write in Spanish and studied Spanish poems and short stories. Lety had left Mexico when she was in third grade. Now her Spanish writing was stuck at that level. She envied Brisa's ability to write in Spanish and spell everything correctly.

"Please take a marker and write your name under the project that interests you and we'll break you up into those groups," Alma said. "Whatever you choose will be your project for the next four weeks. Please only sign up for one project. If you have questions, ask any of us."

Lety hesitated, holding the red marker in her hand. Writing in English was way better than speaking it. With writing, Lety could take her time, think out the vocabulary, and look up words in a dictionary or online. She could cross things out and revise. With speaking, there was no deleting and revising. What came out of your mouth came out! If the other students laughed at your pronunciation or word choice, there was nothing you could do to shove the words back into your mouth.

Kennedy signed her and Brisa's names to the cat hero list.

"Be a cat hero with us," Kennedy said. "We get to make cat toys and other crafts."

Alma walked up to Lety.

"Are you thinking of being our shelter scribe?"

"I don't know." Lety shrugged. "How many profiles do I write?"

"As many as you can in the next four weeks," Alma answered. "The best part is you'll get to work with Dr. V. He'll review all the profiles, so don't worry about misspellings. He'll catch them. Then he'll pass them on to the social media team to post online."

"English isn't my first language," Lety said quietly to Alma.

"Then you should definitely do it. It's a great way to practice."

"Do it!" Brisa exclaimed, clutching Lety's arm. "You are ready for the big time."

Lety gripped her marker tight. At school, Mrs. Camacho helped her with all of her writing assignments. She'd always pull a chair next to Lety's desk and check her writing on the spot. But Mrs. Camacho wasn't here. She was across town, leading summer school. Right now, Aziza, Gazi, Marta, and Santiago were probably playing word splash or hangman to practice vocabulary. Lety loved playing hangman.

With marker in hand, Lety stepped toward the paper that said "Shelter Scribe." Mrs. Camacho wasn't going to be with her everywhere. At some point, she had to be like rocket-blaster Spike and take off to be a hero. Lety uncapped the marker and was about to write her name on the paper when Hunter slipped ahead of her. With a green marker, he wrote his name first.

"Hey!" Lety protested. "I was about to sign my name."

"Looks like you missed the boat," Hunter said with a shrug. "I'm shelter scribe now. Sorry, not sorry."

CHAPTER 3

Big Shoes to Fill

As Hunter stepped away with a smug smile, Lety stood there, confused, trying to understand what he meant by missing the boat. What did a boat have to do with being a shelter scribe?

"What boat?" Lety asked Kennedy and Brisa.

"It's a stupid expression," Kennedy said. "Forget about him."

Lety frowned. She felt like she was back in third grade, clueless about English and not understanding anything again. She glanced over at Hunter. He was talking to Mario Perez, another kid she knew from her school. She thought he was nice. Too nice to be hanging around Hunter.

"Maybe you should change your name to Hunter Fisher if you love *boats* so much!" Brisa shouted, stopping Hunter and Mario mid-conversation. Hunter glared at her.

"Nicely done," Alma said, giving Brisa a fist bump.

As frustrated as Lety felt, she couldn't help but laugh at Brisa's bold comeback.

"Hunter Fisher." Lety chuckled. "Because he likes boats."

Soon, all the girls were cracking up. A spark of hope warmed Lety. Five minutes ago, she didn't know what a shelter scribe was, but now that the possibility of being shelter scribe had opened itself up to her, she wanted to prove to everyone she could do it.

It was like the time in fourth grade when she found *Mrs. Frisby and the Rats of NIMH* at the school library. The ELLs mostly read picture books, but she wanted a book from the fourth-grade bookshelf. She pulled it from the shelf and regretted it immediately. The thickness of the novel made her feel like her head would explode, but once she had it in her hands, she didn't dare put it down. Plus, a few of her classmates were watching her. As she flipped open the book and browsed through the pages, she spotted black-and-white sketches of a tiny mouse, a crow, and supersized rats mixed in with the story. Books with pictures were always a big help to her, and yet this book wasn't for babies. It was perfect. The librarian didn't even question Lety about the reading level. She let Lety check it out and keep it for as long as she needed. When she was done, she decided it was her all-time favorite book.

Now every book in the school library was a friend to her. When she opened them, the words no longer intimidated her; instead they transported her to new worlds, where lab rats could become heroes, and girls from faraway places (like her) could dream in a new language.

Lety raised the marker again, stepped toward the paper, and wrote her name directly beneath Hunter's name.

"She can't do that!" Hunter whined.

"Come here, you two," Alma said with a roll of her eyes. Hunter and Lety shuffled toward Alma until they were in front of her. "Look, I'm happy to announce that we now have two shelter scribes! Isn't it exciting?" Alma clasped her hands. Hunter's face twisted. "You are going to work together —"

"Augh!" Hunter grunted, interrupting Alma.

"Don't be rude, Hunter," Kennedy hissed. Lety felt like she'd just been tripped. What was Hunter's problem?

"Anyway," Alma continued. "Together, you'll both write ten profiles. And no pressure, but you should realize that you have big shoes to fill."

Lety looked down at her sandals, confused. Hunter caught her doing it and scoffed.

"Our last shelter scribe, Gaby, was like J.K. Rowling, okay?" Alma continued. "She wrote fast and every story was pure gold. As soon as Gaby created a profile for a furry friend, it was adopted within days."

"Not even days, hours!" another volunteer chimed in.

Alma nodded. "He's right."

"I already read and write at high school level, so it's no problem," Hunter bragged.

"You do not," Kennedy said, shaking her head. "Stop lying, Hunter."

"It's true," Mario jumped in. "Our teacher said so. You guys aren't in Mrs. Morgan's class, so you don't know."

"Stop taking his side, Mario," Kennedy snapped.

Lety swallowed hard as a wave of worry swept over her. Could Hunter really write at the high school level? She looked at Alma, who seemed to be enjoying the fireworks between Kennedy and Mario.

"Alma, how do we know which animals to write for?" Lety asked.

"I'll get a list from Dr. V. I'll have it tomorrow for you guys, okay?"

Alma turned to leave. Once she was out of earshot, Hunter adjusted his baseball cap and stepped closer to Lety.

"I think you should just let me write all the profiles. I mean, I can get them done fast and they'll be awesome." Hunter shrugged. "Plus, I know you're still learning English. It might be too hard for you."

Brisa put her arm protectively around Lety's shoulders.

"You heard Alma; she says there are two shelter scribes," Brisa said. "Not one. Two. *Dos.*"

Hunter shook his head. "I just want to do what's best for the animals."

"Oh, you just want to do what's best for the animals? How sweet!" Kennedy mocked. "Give me a break." She rolled her eyes.

"I have an idea!" Mario exclaimed. "We can have a contest."

Lety's stomach twisted into a knot.

"I like it!" Hunter said. "We can prove who the best shelter scribe is."

"That's dumb!" Kennedy said.

"It's not about proving who's the best writer. It's about the animals," Mario said in a calm, low voice. "If you really cared about the animals here at the shelter, wouldn't you want them to be adopted as soon as possible, Lety?"

"Of course I do," she said softly.

"Then shouldn't the animals have the best person writing for them? The contest is the fairest way to find out who should be shelter scribe. You heard what Alma said. The last shelter scribe was like J.K. Rowling and —"

"So what?" Kennedy interrupted. "They're writing animal profiles, not playing a game of Quidditch, Mario."

Mario palm-slapped his face in frustration. "Kennedy, you're driving me nuts. If you'd listen for a minute, you'd see that my point is that the best writer should be shelter scribe. We need an easy and fair way to determine who that is."

Lety took a deep breath to suck in the words and process everything Mario was saying. The best writer? Easy and fair? None of it seemed fair to her. She wondered why Hunter and Mario were making this so complicated. Then the answer came to her. It was like everything back at school. The other kids, the non-ELLs, never invited them to birthday parties or to participate in their group projects. This contest felt like another way to exclude her. It made her angry.

"Fine," Lety said with more attitude than she wanted. "Who'll decide on the best shelter scribe? Dr. Villalobos? Alma?"

"No! We can't tell them anything," Mario said. He stepped closer to the group and lowered his voice. "Listen. I heard from one of the other volunteers that their former shelter scribe, Gaby, got in trouble and wasn't allowed to play with the dogs and cats again. Dr. Villalobos almost kicked her out of the shelter."

"Kicked out?" Lety asked.

"I can't get kicked out. My grandma will flip her lid," Hunter said.

"But Alma said Gaby was awesome," Brisa added.

"Hey, that's what I heard. Anyway, we don't want that to happen, right? If Dr. V. could do that to the last shelter scribe . . . I mean, he could kick us out of camp, too, for making this a contest."

"We have to agree to keep it just between us, okay?" Hunter said.

Lety nodded.

"The winner will be based on adoptions," Mario said. "Alma said that she needed ten profiles . . . that means you guys each write five. She also said that as soon as you have them done, the social media team will post them online. I'm signed up for that. I'll make sure they go up as fast as lightning. Whoever has more dogs or cats adopted from the five by the end of week two is our shelter scribe. The loser has to do something else, like volunteer in the pantry." Mario gestured toward the Food Pantry Hero sign taped up on the wall. There wasn't a single name on it. "No one has signed up, so they'll want the help."

"That's because it smells," Kennedy said. "Like you guys."

"Do we have a deal or not?" Mario said, ignoring Kennedy's insult.

"Five profiles?" Lety asked. Mario and Hunter nodded. Lety wanted more than anything to help dogs like Spike and all the rest of the animals find forever families, but five profiles in two weeks seemed impossible. As if sensing Lety's anxiety, Kennedy blazed her light blue eyes on Mario.

"Hold your horses! You don't get to make up all the rules," she said. "I think we should make this more of a challenge for Hunter since he claims that he writes at the high school level."

"Fine with me," Hunter said.

"What do you have in mind?" Mario asked.

"We'll give you five words that you have to use for the profiles," Kennedy said. "This will make it more fair since you're so advanced or whatever."

Lety pulled Kennedy's elbow to whisper into her ear.

"Kennedy, I don't know if we should —"

"Trust me, Lety."

She trusted Kennedy with her whole heart, but by giving Hunter an extra challenge, she worried that it made the contest uneven. Now, if she — by some great miracle — pulled it off and won, Hunter would say it was because he had tougher words. She wanted to be shelter scribe fair and square.

"What do you say?" Kennedy asked.

"Deal! May the best shelter scribe win," Hunter said, holding his hand out for Lety to shake. Lety shook it.

"Tomorrow, bring your five words," Mario said. "No backing down."

With that, the two boys turned to leave.

"This is going to be like the Hulk versus an ant," Hunter said loudly to Mario as they walked away. Lety looked back at him. Their eyes met. She wanted him to know she heard him refer to her as an insect. Hunter suddenly stomped on the floor. "Splat! Game over!" The two boys laughed.

Chapter 4

Adios, Spike

Brisa gathered Lety and Kennedy into a huddle.

"We need big words, *chicas*," she said.

"High-school-level words, for sure," Kennedy added, pulling her phone from her back pocket. "I'll google some and I can ask my big brother. He'll know . . ." Kennedy stopped and looked over at Lety, who was silent. "Are you okay?"

30

Lety stood motionless as a rush of English words flooded her head. One word in particular stood out among them all: *doubt*.

Doubt was a word she knew well in English and Spanish. In Spanish, doubt was *duda*. Doubt had followed her all the way from Mexico to the United States. It was there on her first day of school when she couldn't understand a word the teacher said. It was there when some older boys sent her to the boys' bathroom instead of the girls' bathroom and then laughed at her every time they saw her in the hallway. She never thought she'd learn English, let alone make any friends at school. Though she did both, doubt had never left her side.

A loud commotion of barking and kids rushing to the door snapped Lety out of her daze.

"Everyone, Spike is leaving," Alma announced, holding Spike in her arms. "Come and say good-bye."

All of the kids gathered around Alma. Hunter leaned in to give Spike a quick kiss on his head. It was hard to stay mad at him when he could give Spike such a sweet kiss. As the group said their good-byes and moved on, Lety approached with Brisa and Kennedy.

"Let's make a little good-bye prayer for him. Lety, can you?" Brisa said.

"That's a good idea. Spike needs all the prayers he can get," Alma said, and handed Spike to Lety.

Lety gave Spike a gentle squeeze and closed her eyes. Brisa and Kennedy followed.

"Dear Saint Francis, you loved all of God's creatures," Lety began. "We ask you to please watch over Spike. He is a hero that saved a baby girl. Now he is going to a foster home and we pray he will be safe, loved, and fed the best —"

"Real *carne*!" Brisa interrupted excitedly.

"Yes, that he will have real steak," Lety added. "And please make sure he always has a toy to chew. Amen."

"Amen," the three girls repeated.

Lety gave Spike a kiss on his head. She wished so much he could be her dog. She wished so much that he was going home with her.

"I can tell already that you're going to be an awesome shelter scribe," Alma said with a wink before taking Spike from her and whisking him out of the room.

After Alma's kinds words and Spike being whisked away, the room swirled with chatter and activity. Brisa and Kennedy joined the other cat heroes. Hunter and Mario were reading the animal profiles posted on the bulletin board. Still, Lety stood frozen. Spike's departure had made the contest more urgent to her. Had she really agreed to be a shelter scribe and compete with Hunter Farmer, the fifth grader who read and wrote at a high school level?

She thought back to her own words to Dr. Villalobos: *Sometimes people or pets that are not wanted can still become heroes — if we give them a chance.*

If Hunter thought he was going to splat her like an ant in this contest, she was going to prove him wrong. She owed it to the hero dog Spike, and the hat-hating Finn, and all of the furry friends needing a forever family to squash the doubt and write profiles that were pure gold.

CHAPTER 5

Five English Words

When Brisa's mom dropped Lety off at her home, her seven-year-old brother, Eddie, was sitting on the front porch waiting for her.

"Lety! Lety!" he sang, rushing from the porch to unlatch the gate for her. "You missed the best day ever!"

"You played hangman, right?"

"With chalk on the playground and I knew all the words."

"Smarty-pants," Lety said, opening the screen door for her brother. The minute she walked in, she could smell the spicy aroma of lentil soup from the kitchen.

"Mrs. Camacho let me help the new kids. There's Luis from Guatemala and Zeenat from . . . I don't remember, but I got to be their buddies. We had *paletas*. And tomorrow, we have to bring in pictures of our families. Will you help me find one?"

"Sure," Lety said. She passed the dining table toward the kitchen to greet her mom but stopped once she spotted a stack of paint swatches. It was her mom's tradition to bring her one swatch from every paint job, but this time there were at least a dozen stacked on the table. Each one, the size of a bookmark, featured several shades of purple and pink.

"Did you know there were so many purples, Lety?" Eddie asked, taking a seat at the table.

Lety shuffled through them and shook her head.

"I did," Eddie said. "I know all the colors already. Velvet violet, marvelous mauve, spring lavender . . ."

While Eddie rattled off a list of purple paints, Lety's mom walked into the room with a pot of soup. She placed it on the table and gave Lety a hug.

"*¿Te gustan?*" she asked, lowering her eyes to the swatches Lety held in her hands.

"*Sí, son hermosas. Gracias!*" Lety said.

Lety's mom had been an artist in Mexico who sold her paintings of birds, stray animals, and flowers in the main plaza of Tlaquepaque. Now she painted homes and apartments. Most people wanted their walls painted colors that her mom called *sencillos*, like beige, gray, and creamy whites, but she always picked up the most vibrant paint swatches for Lety. Lety and Eddie studied the colors and practiced pronouncing them every night.

It always impressed Mrs. Camacho when Lety would describe colors not just as blue or green but instead as indigo blue or moss green. In this way, Lety felt her English was improving, but she wasn't sure that knowing names for different paint colors would help her now as shelter scribe. Knowing paint colors certainly didn't help her mom when they went to her first parent-teacher conference. Lety's mom and teacher sat across from each other and traded silent smiles for ten minutes — it felt like forever to Lety — until a translator arrived.

With Mrs. Camacho, things were a lot easier. She spoke Spanish, but she didn't speak Aziza or Gazi's language. Last year, when Lety witnessed Mrs. Camacho struggling to communicate with Gazi's parents about a permission slip needed for a field trip, Lety recognized the deep scarlet shade of embarrassment that flooded Gazi's face. From that day forward, she always made sure Gazi was never sent to the wrong bathroom or left to eat alone in the lunchroom.

"How go first day of camp?" Lety's mom asked, making Eddie grin.

"You're speaking English!" Eddie said. Lety's mom smiled back at him.

"I learn English, too." She winked at him. "I'm best student." Eddie shook his head, still cracking up.

"*¿Y? ¿Como te fue, Lety?*" she asked Lety again.

"Good. I volunteered to be a shelter scribe," Lety answered. Her mom winced and Lety quickly translated for her. "*Me fue muy bien. Voy a escribir historias para las mascotas —*" Lety started before Eddie interrupted.

"Cool!" Eddie exclaimed. "Can we get a dog?"

"I hope so. I met a sweet dog today that would be perfect for us."

"*¿Como se llama?*" Lety's mom asked.

"Spike."

Lety's mom laughed.

"That's a cool name!" Eddie said.

"Maybe we can bring him home?" Lety asked her mom.

Lety's mom shifted her head from left to right as if thinking it over.

"No se," she answered. *"Hablaré con su papá."*

"Gracias, Mamita,*"* Lety said, grateful that her mom was willing to talk to her father. It was a good sign that her mom liked the idea of having a dog.

"You have to say 'thank you,' Lety," Eddie said. "We won't learn English if we always speak Spanish. That's what Mrs. Camacho says."

"She also says we shouldn't lose our Spanish, Eddie," Lety said. "That's important, too. We don't have to choose one or the other. The goal is to be bilingual."

Eddie shrugged. "We already are, but I'm going to be more than bilingual. I will learn all the languages in the whole world! So Mom has to learn them, too. English most of all."

"Aye, Eddie," Lety said, shaking her head. "She's learning as fast as she can."

"I know," he said, and then got up and kissed his mom on the cheek. "I know you're trying, Mamita."

Lety smiled at her brother and thought back to Eddie's choir performance last Christmas. After the event, parents and teachers mingled in the school cafeteria. As she and Eddie bounced around, chatting with their friends and teachers, her mom huddled close with Brisa's mom. Both of them were too shy to meet other parents with the little English they spoke. Maybe her brother was right. Deep down, Lety wanted what he wanted. She wanted her mom to be able to join conversations instead of standing in the back of the room scared to speak and say the wrong thing. Lety understood how that felt.

Later that night when her father came home from work, Lety and Eddie kept him company at the dinner table. They made it a family practice to do their homework and drink a glass of milk while he ate his dinner.

Lety flipped through an English dictionary to find words that would be at Hunter's high school reading level. Kennedy and Brisa had said they'd also help her come up with words. Lety hoped they were having more luck. Eddie browsed through a family photo album for a picture to take to his summer ELL class the next day. She looked over at her father as he cut a piece of pork on his plate and scooped it up with a corn tortilla.

"Papá, do you know any hard English words?" she asked. "I need five words for tomorrow." He arched his eyebrows at her and wiped his mouth with a paper towel.

"Todas son difíciles para mí, mija," he said, and scooped up some more pork.

"If you find difficult words, write them down and practice them," Eddie said, dipping a chocolate chip cookie into his glass of milk. "That's what Mrs. Camacho says."

Lety's father frowned. Her father rarely spoke English, but he understood everything.

"I can study the difficult words with you, Papá. I will be the teacher since I know English best," Eddie said. Lety laughed at her brother, but it was true. For Eddie, English came so easily. Mrs. Camacho said it was because Eddie started learning English at a younger age. She said young brains are like sponges, absorbing new languages easily. Lety wished she could make her brain a sponge, too.

Their father leaned over and proudly patted Eddie's head. Lety's father had been the first to come to the United States. He came to work construction with an uncle who had started his own business years ago. Her father was gone for an entire year. Every day her father was gone, Lety worried. She yearned for his voice in the morning, singing a song from the radio, and his boots at the door before they went to sleep. During that year, her mom, Eddie, and Lety lived with their grandparents to save money for their trip to the United States. Eddie barely remembered anything from that time — he was too young — but Lety felt the emptiness of their dad's departure and the anxiety as they waited for the call to join him in a new country. When her dad and uncle had finally earned enough money to send for them, they filled their backpacks and left their home in Tlaquepaque for good.

Lety's father stood up from the table to take his plate to the kitchen, but before he did, he leaned down and planted a kiss on Lety's head. *"Tu estudias."* He tapped a finger on her dictionary. *"Yo trabajo."*

"Papá, you have to study, too," Eddie said. "Not just work all the time." Lety passed him a stern look to be quiet.

"He works all day so that we can study," Lety explained.

"Tiene razon," Lety's mother said in agreement.

"After English, I'm going to learn Italian so I can surprise my soccer coach," Eddie chirped. "Then maybe Farsi or Tagalog. There are so many languages. Thousands! English is my favorite, though."

"Que bueno, mijo," Lety's mom said, pouring him more milk.

"I can barely come up with five good English words," Lety said, staring down at the dictionary. Her mom put a hand on Lety's shoulder.

"I do not know so many words," her mom said. *"Lo siento, mija."*

"It's okay, Kennedy and Brisa are helping me."

"Use one of these," Eddie said, sliding a paint swatch with five different shades of pink on it across the table toward her. "These are good."

Lety closed the dictionary. She studied the paint swatch and slipped it into her book bag while Eddie moved into the living room to watch a cartoon called *Zombie Cats*. She joined him on the couch, but once their father came in and took his place on the corner of the couch, he switched the channel to a Spanish game show.

Eddie groaned and dropped down to the floor with a sulk. Lety curled up next to her dad. The game show was called *Cien mexicanos dicen*. It was the Mexican version of *Family Feud*, where two families were pitted against each other to answer questions about everyday topics. Lety looked forward to the show because the host was funny and the families could win thousands of dollars. She liked to daydream that it was her family on the show winning fifty thousand bucks. The big prize wasn't the only reason she liked the show. It was her favorite show because of the way her father's stern mouth curved into a smile whenever the host made a joke. Tonight, the host asked the families to name something they never left home without. One by one, the contestants guessed wallet, cell phone, eyeglasses, purse, and a variety of wrong answers.

"*Identificación,*" her father guessed.

"ID," Eddie repeated.

Hearing her tired father come alive after a long day of work comforted Lety. Her mom joined them on the couch and patted Lety's leg.

"*Papeles,*" Lety's mom shouted at the television as soon as she sat down. Lety looked down at her mother's chipped fingernails, covered with splotches of cream-colored paint. And even though her mom usually wore a bandanna over her hair when she painted homes, Lety could see flecks of ivory white on a few strands of her mom's brown hair. Her father had showered and changed into clean clothes as soon as he arrived home, but Lety could still smell the earthy aroma of a new construction project soaked into his dark hair and golden-brown skin.

"Identification," Lety yelled out. "Why aren't they guessing that?"

A shrill buzzer rang out on the show, signaling that the

family had struck out. Now the other family had the chance to guess the remaining answer. They huddled close before shouting the winning answer: driver's license/identification.

Lety's dad smiled wide. *"Lo sabía."*

"That family should have listened to us, Lety," Eddie said. "We knew the answer."

"We knew the answer in two languages," Lety said. "We would have won the big prize."

ChapteR 6

Fair and Square

"Lety! Brisa!" Kennedy screamed in panic when they walked into the multipurpose room. She rushed up to them with a paper in her hand. "Hunter and Mario say that we agreed yesterday that they would give you five words, too. I don't remember agreeing to that," Kennedy said, glaring at the two boys.

"*¡¿Que?!*" Brisa exclaimed. "No way!" she said, raising a finger at the sky.

"Are those their words?" Lety asked, grabbing the paper from Kennedy's hands. Kennedy nodded.

"They're ridiculous," Kennedy said just as the boys joined them.

"She agreed to it," Mario said. "You can't change the rules."

"You are the rule changers," Brisa sniped.

Lety scanned the five words Hunter had picked for her to use in the animal profiles. A lump formed in her throat. She wasn't familiar with any of them. They were from another universe as far as she was concerned. Kennedy snatched the paper from Lety's hands and waved it accusingly at Hunter and Mario.

"C'mon! 'Supersonic'? 'Infectious'? 'Rigid'? Where did you get these stupid words? And how is Lety supposed to use 'colossal' and 'fusion' in the animal profiles?"

"You don't play fair, Hunter," Brisa added.

"How am I not being fair?" Hunter said. He grasped the baseball hat on his head in exasperation. "You get to choose words for me, but I'm not allowed to pick words for you?"

"You're the one that bragged about writing at a high school level," Kennedy said.

"Can I see the words you have for me?" Hunter said to Lety, ignoring Kennedy's scowl.

Lety pulled her book bag off and dipped her hands into a side pocket for the paint swatch. Kennedy and Brisa also pulled out small notepads with scribbled words.

"Your first word is 'rambunctious,'" Kennedy said.

"Easy enough," Hunter said with a shrug, and jotted it down on his phone.

"'Gush' and 'beckon,'" Brisa offered.

"More easy words," Hunter said, and scoffed.

"Seriously, Hunter?" Kennedy said.

"How about 'scrumptious'?" Brisa added. "I love how that word sounds. Don't you? Good luck using it, Hunter."

"Easiest word in the world."

"'Cerise,'" Lety said. Hunter's smug smile twisted into a frown.

"Is that even a real word? That doesn't sound like English," he said. "We have to use English words."

"It is English," Lety said. "It is a deep pink color. I have it here." She showed him the paint swatch. "See? Sweet Cerise."

"I don't think so. Give him another word," Mario said.

"It sounds like *cereza*, which is 'cherry' in Spanish, but 'cerise' is an English word," Lety said.

"I don't think it should count," Hunter said to Mario. "It sounds Spanish or French."

"Oh, because you don't use any Spanish-sounding words?" Kennedy snapped. "Last year, you had a piñata birthday party. With the robot piñata, remember? Where do you think 'piñata' comes from?"

Lety and Brisa exchanged a look of surprise. They were used to not being invited to classmates' birthday parties, unless it was an ELL student's party, but they didn't know about Hunter's piñata party. Nor that Kennedy had gone to it. She had never mentioned it to them.

"It's a borrowed Spanish word, or did you not learn that in all those high-school-level books you supposedly read?" Kennedy said with so much snarky attitude that Hunter's face turned cherry red.

"Okay, fine. Whatever," Hunter said with a shrug. He directed his gaze at Lety. "I'll use your words. Do you agree to use our five words in the animal profiles, then?"

"That wasn't part of the deal, you guys," Kennedy said, crossing her arms over her chest. "Lety, you don't have to agree to anything. We can go have a conversation with Dr. Villalobos right now about this whole shelter scribe contest."

Mario gasped. "You can't do that!"

"We might get kicked out, and my grandma paid a lot for this camp," Hunter said. "So don't even think about it, Kennedy."

Lety wanted to say that her family paid a lot, too, but she didn't want to sound like a copycat, repeating anything Hunter said.

"You should think about that before you make up new rules, then," Kennedy said.

Lety felt like she was in a Mexican telenovela where all the characters are in the courtroom. In this episode, Kennedy was a fearless lawyer defending Lety. On the other side of the court stood the villains: Hunter and Mario. Yet Lety didn't feel like the victim needing defending. Even though the words Hunter came up with seemed impossible, Lety wanted the chance to compete with Hunter fair and square. If she won, she'd win because she helped the shelter's dogs and cats find their forever homes. She gathered the words she wanted to say in her brain and spoke up.

"We're not going to tell," Lety said with a quick nod to Kennedy. "I'll use their words, okay? Now let's get to work."

CHAPTER 7

Not His Dog Anymore

Alma held a piece of yellow tablet paper with the names of ten dogs and cats. "Here you go," she said, handing the paper to Lety. "Remember, no longer than a hundred words. Dr. V. likes sweet and simple."

"We got it," Hunter said.

"Sweet and simple," Lety repeated, liking how those words sounded together.

"Good luck!" Alma said, walking off to talk to some other volunteers.

As soon as Alma was out of earshot, Lety gave the paper to Mario. With one quick rip, he passed both Lety and Hunter a list of five furry friends.

"May the best shelter scribe win," he said.

Hunter dashed off with his list. Lety remained still, gazing over the names of her own furry friends. Her list included three cats named Chicharito, Lorca, and Bandit, and two dogs: Finn and a tiny Pomeranian mix named Bella. Brisa and Kennedy hovered close to her to see who she had.

"Oh, look! You get to write about that cute hat-hating dog," Brisa said excitedly. "I wish I could help you, but we are making — what do you call it, Kennedy?"

"Catnip pouches," Kennedy answered.

"Catnip pouches! So much fun," Brisa said, pulling on Lety's hand. "Where will you go?"

"I will start with Finn," Lety said. "But I'll go to the cat room later, okay?"

"*¡Hasta luego, capitán!*" Brisa said, turning on a thicker than usual Bolivian accent for extra drama. Lety giggled. Over the past three years, Lety had managed to lose most of her Mexican accent, shedding it as fast as she could, like it was an itchy polyester sweater. Brisa, on the other hand, clung to her Bolivian accent like it was the world's softest sweater made from silky alpaca fleece. Once, when Mrs. Camacho corrected Brisa's accent, Brisa quickly defended herself. She explained that her accent was her grandma's accent and it was all she had left of Bolivia. She didn't want to give it up, too. Mrs. Camacho smiled and nodded, "You hang on to that beautiful accent, Brisa Quispe!"

As the girls parted ways, it struck Lety that this was one of the few times this year she'd been without Brisa or Kennedy at her side. So far, all her summer days had been spent with them at Kennedy's neighborhood pool. Brisa's mom picked up Lety every day for the pool and camp. Now Lety was on her own. For a moment, she second-guessed herself, wondering if it would have been easier to have just avoided the competition with Hunter and signed up to be a cat hero with her best friends. Was proving she could be a shelter scribe and write as well as him that important?

"Everything cool, Lety?" Alma asked her. "You're sort of zoning out."

Lety looked up, surprised to find Alma there. She pocketed her list.

"I'm just thinking about what I'll write for Finn," she answered, followed by a nervous giggle.

"Take this for help." Alma handed Lety a flyer with Spike's picture on it. "Gaby wrote it. You can use it as an example."

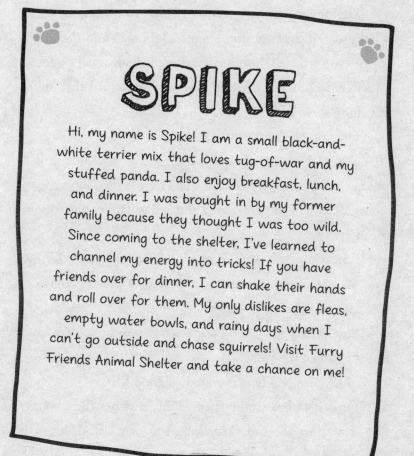

SPIKE

Hi, my name is Spike! I am a small black-and-white terrier mix that loves tug-of-war and my stuffed panda. I also enjoy breakfast, lunch, and dinner. I was brought in by my former family because they thought I was too wild. Since coming to the shelter, I've learned to channel my energy into tricks! If you have friends over for dinner, I can shake their hands and roll over for them. My only dislikes are fleas, empty water bowls, and rainy days when I can't go outside and chase squirrels! Visit Furry Friends Animal Shelter and take a chance on me!

Lety quickly read it and laughed at the part where it said Spike disliked rainy days when he couldn't go outside to chase squirrels.

"Do you think Spike will be back?" Lety asked, already missing sweet Spike.

"Definitely," Alma answered. "He always comes back. That's sort of the problem. People adopt him and then they say he's too wild. I'll never understand it. I love that dog, but I can't have him because we have a cat now and they don't get along so well."

"Did you get your cat from here?"

"Yep! Her name is Feather. She's a beauty." Alma pulled out her cell phone. "Check her out." Lety leaned in to see an image of a majestic gray, tan, and white tabby with bright green eyes.

"Emerald-green eyes," Lety said. "She is so beautiful."

"She's the best cat ever, but she doesn't tolerate dogs."

"Can anyone adopt Spike?"

"Sure, as long as Dr. Villalobos believes that you're kind and a good fit for Spike."

"How does he know if you are a good fit?"

"Dr. Villalobos studies people. He watches their behavior. How they act and everything they say. He thinks I'm super awesome, so obviously he's an excellent judge of character."

Lety felt suddenly warm listening to Alma. She had a terrible thought: If Dr. Villalobos found out about the contest, would he think she wasn't fit to adopt Spike? They were supposed to be working together. She thought back to what Mario had said earlier about Gaby almost being kicked out from volunteering at the shelter. Lety didn't want to be kicked out. She wanted to be the best shelter scribe ever and help the animals. She also wanted to adopt sweet Spike.

"That was a joke," Alma said. "You okay, *chica*?"

For a second Lety considered asking Alma if it was true what Mario said about Gaby being kicked out, but she shoved the idea away. Alma was smart. She'd start to wonder why Lety was worried about being kicked out and maybe bust them all. "I think you are awesome, too."

"Thanks, *chica*," Alma said with a big smile. "You're not so bad yourself. Are you interested in Spike? Being his forever family?"

"Yes, but my mom has to talk to my dad about it."

"Does he like dogs?"

"Oh yes. Very much. When we lived in Mexico, he used to share his breakfast with the stray dogs. He even once built a doghouse for a neighbor. We were going to get a dog, but then he moved here and we came later."

"I know I just met you, but you seem like a good fit for Spike. Still, I'm not the one who decides. Dr. Villalobos is the one you have to impress."

"I'll try my best," Lety said. "Thanks."

She rushed off toward the Bow Wow Zone. When she arrived, Hunter was already there. He stood motionless in front of a cage, as if mesmerized by the dog inside. Lety passed behind him toward Finn's cage, but Hunter never budged. He remained standing and staring at the large white dog. He didn't notice her.

"Hunter?" Lety said. "Are you okay?"

Hunter snapped out of his daze and looked at Lety with sad, light brown eyes.

"He looks like my dog," Hunter said, gesturing at the white Great Pyrenees/Labrador mixed-breed dog who was chewing on a squeaky toy. "I mean, she's not my dog anymore. She . . ." Hunter's voice lowered and drifted off like he wasn't sure he should say any more. He continued to gaze at the dog.

"She's not your dog anymore?" Lety asked softly. "What happened?"

Hunter shrugged.

Lety had only been at camp with Hunter for two days now, but she noticed he shrugged a lot. Brisa had already nicknamed him Mr. Shruggy Llama. The nickname made Lety laugh, but now she recognized something hidden behind Hunter's shrugs. Something so sad that not even words could express it. Lety was good at reading facial gestures, body language, and tone of voice. For her first year at school, these clues guided her and helped her learn English. She knew that Hunter's shrugs were meant to express that he didn't care or didn't know, but the shrugs were also replacing something that he did care about. Lety was certain it had something to do with his dog that wasn't his dog anymore.

Hunter stayed silent, not answering Lety's question. She decided to try one more time.

"What was your dog's name?"

"Gunner," Hunter answered, still focused on the dog in the cage. Lety glanced over at Finn, who was wagging his tail and looking up at her with golden-brown eyes. She gave him a quick wink to let him know she'd be back. As she joined Hunter in front of the furry white dog's cage, Finn whined.

"Gunner," she said. "That's cute. Am I saying it right?"

Hunter nodded. On the cage was a sheet of paper listing some facts about Sawyer, the white Pyrenees/Labrador. Lety looked over his age, breed, and intake date, which was the date he was brought into the shelter.

"Poor Sawyer. He has been here since March. Five months! Why hasn't anyone adopted him? He is so cute."

Hunter shrugged.

"People are dumb," he mumbled.

Lety wondered if he thought she was dumb. She clapped her hands at Sawyer, who immediately dropped his toy and walked up and pawed at the clear plastic barrier between them. "Hello, sweet boy!" She squatted down to be at eye level with him. "You're a pretty boy! Yes, you are!"

Hunter squatted down next to her, and Lety noticed light brown freckles scattered over Hunter's cheeks like a connect-the-dots game.

"He's just like my dog, except that Gunner was a full-breed Great Pyrenees," Hunter said. "She had a few little gray strands around her face, but mostly she was fluffy white like this one. I got her for my fifth birthday. She was just a puppy."

"How cute."

"She looked like a white bear," Hunter said with a nod. "She was smart, too."

Lety liked the way Hunter talked about his dog. When he spoke about her, his voice became as soft as Sawyer's white furry coat and his brown eyes as glossy as Sawyer's wet nose.

"Do you know what you'll write?" Lety asked.

"I've got some ideas," Hunter said. He opened his notebook and uncapped his pen. Finn let out a long impatient whine, and they both laughed.

"Sorry, Finn! I'm coming!" Lety yelled, and stood up. Now Sawyer barked, as if pleading for her to stay and call him sweet names. "Sweet fluffy boy, Hunter will stay with you. He's going to write you an awesome profile."

A faint smile crossed Hunter's face. Lety walked back to Finn's cage and jotted down notes on her small notepad. She stopped and glanced at Hunter. He remained on the floor across from Sawyer. His notebook was open and his pen raced across and down the page with furious speed. She envied how easy it was for him. She wondered if Hunter could really read at a high school level and if she'd ever be able to write as fast as him someday.

CHAPTER 8

Sawyer Beckons

"It's amazing," Kennedy said, after reading Hunter's animal profile for the large Great Pyrenees/Labrador. The next day, the profile was already printed with a photograph of Sawyer and pinned up on the bulletin board in the shelter's reception area. "But there's no way I'm telling him that."

"He used 'beckon,'" Brisa said softly. "Maybe he writes at the high school level like he said? *¿Qué piensas,* Lety?"

"I think maybe he does," she said, taking a deep breath before reading the profile.

SAWYER

Does my easygoing name beckon you to adopt me? No? Not yet? Let me share a little more: I'm a two-year-old Great Pyrenees/Labrador mix with the best qualities of both dog breeds. The Pyrenees side is protective and a loving family dog. The Labrador side will want to get you on your feet for a run or a long walk along the lake. Hey, I'll even jump into the lake! I'm a great swimmer. I'm housetrained, too, but be patient as I settle into my new home. Visit me at Furry Friends Animal Shelter today!

"It is good," Lety said. "It sounds just like Sawyer."

"Mario told me that Hunter is almost done with Scout's and Kenzie's profiles, too," Kennedy said. "How far along are you?"

Lety's head swirled. So far, she had only started Finn's profile.

"I'm going to finish Finn today, and then I'll move on to Bella's profile and then the cats'."

"You have to get more done before the weekend. Weekends are big for adoptions. It's your best chance to win," Kennedy said. "Can you get at least three done? You could complete the last two over the weekend at the pool with us and have them ready on Monday. What do you think?"

"No pressure!" Brisa joked.

Lety swallowed hard. Dr. Villalobos suddenly called everyone to take a seat.

"Today we're going to watch a film about dog aggression and how to behave if you're ever confronted with a hostile dog."

Lety scooted her chair next to Brisa and Kennedy. She glanced at Hunter. From under his baseball cap, Hunter gave her a quick smile. She smiled back.

Dr. V. folded up one of his long sleeves and went around showing everyone a bite-sized scar on his arm with the date of 08/16/97 around it. "See this scar?"

Some of the kids made yuck noises at the scar, while Mario rolled up his pant leg to show off his own scar.

"Skateboard injury," Mario explained. Dr. V. grimaced and told him to use kneepads. Everyone laughed.

"I got this scar when I was in college," Dr. V. said. "I was on my morning jog when a full-grown Doberman jumped out at me. Luckily, he just got my arm, and I was able to call for help and get free with no more than this ugly gash."

"Did it hurt?" Kennedy asked.

"Oh yeah! It hurt like the dickens!"

Lety and Brisa passed each other clueless looks. They had never heard of anything hurting "like the dickens" before. Lety hoped she never felt anything that hurt like the dickens. It didn't sound good.

"Animal shelters like ours are full of fluffy sweet kittens and playful adorable dogs, but unfortunately not all dogs have been socialized to be good dogs. Some dogs behave aggressively because they've been neglected and abused or raised that way by humans. If ever you're confronted with one, I want you to know what to do," Dr. Villalobos said.

"He is nice," Brisa said as Dr. V. switched on a video.

The film started by showing dogs in various stages of aggression, displaying sharp teeth and letting out low growls. Lety pulled out Finn's profile. He definitely *was not* an aggressive dog. Finn was sweet and mostly quiet until someone wore a hat, but she didn't want to mention his hat-hating ways in the profile. She worried it would scare people away from adopting him. Instead she described Finn's favorite blue blanket and noted his age and breed. She still needed to use one of the five words in his profile. She grabbed her dictionary and looked up *colossal* and *fusion*. Neither worked. She looked up *infectious*, *rigid*, and *supersonic*. She frowned and closed her dictionary just as the man in the film was giving tips on how to act when faced with an angry dog.

"Don't move; stand rigid and be silent," the man advised. "Most importantly, do not make eye contact with an angry dog, as it will see that as a challenge."

Rigid! It was one of the words she was supposed to include in a profile.

The man in the video had used *rigid* to mean stiff, but it also could mean being strict about rules. Lety's brain buzzed as she finally saw a way to fit *rigid* into the profile. She jotted down a few more notes about his favorite blanket. It was a soft blue fleece blanket that he dragged in his mouth from one corner of his cage to the other. After a few minutes, Finn's profile was finished.

FINN

I am a sweet two-year-old Labrador/shepherd that gets along well with other dogs and people. At the shelter, I sleep on a periwinkle-blue blanket, but I am not rigid about where I sleep. I will happily give up my favorite blanket to sleep at your home (my new fur-ever home!) and cuddle close to you. Visit me today at the Furry Friends Animal Shelter!

CHAPTER 9

A Strong Cool Wind

The next day, three new profiles were up on the Furry Friends Animal Shelter website. Hunter had finished a profile for Kenzie, the tan-and-white American pit bull.

"He used 'gush,'" Kennedy announced. "I didn't think he'd find a way, but he did." The three girls huddled over a computer at the reception desk to view Kenzie's profile on the shelter's website.

KENZIE

Hi! I'm a four-year-old American pit bull mix. When people find out that I'm part pit bull, they walk straight past my cage. Even though I do my best to sit up straight and show off my big brown eyes, they don't stop to say hello. Will you pass me by, too? If you stop, you'll see that I'm gentle and smart. The shelter staff gushes over me because I'm housetrained and I've mastered walking on a leash. They also say I'm a patient girl, but I can't wait to meet you! Visit me at Furry Friends Animal Shelter today!

A wave of mixed emotions flooded over Lety. Once again, Hunter had written a beautiful profile. She was glad because it meant that someone would hopefully adopt Kenzie soon. Yet Lety felt like she was letting Kennedy and Brisa down. More than that, she felt like she was letting the shelter down. She pulled out the profile she'd started on Bella, the fluffy black Pomeranian.

"I don't know why I thought I could be shelter scribe," she mumbled.

"Your profile for Finn was awesome. You just need to write them faster," Kennedy said. "It's Friday already. You need to get as many profiles up as possible today for the weekend." Kennedy looked at her watch. "C'mon, Brisa, we have to go help make feather toys."

"Be there in a second," Brisa said, hanging back with Lety as Kennedy walked off toward the multipurpose room.

"I think she's mad at me," Lety said.

"No, she's not. She just really wants you to beat Mr. Shruggy Llama and Mario. It's Kennedy. She doesn't like to lose. Remember that soccer match we played against Mario's team and he accused her of a handball?"

Lety nodded; she remembered the game. "We won that game. Why is she holding a grudge?"

"We are talking about Kennedy and Mario. They are like two stubborn goats." Brisa shook her head. "Enough about them. I have to go to the cat room, but first I want to talk because you have this *loca* look in your eyes like you want to quit. I hear it in your voice, too."

Lety wondered how Brisa became such a great mind reader. Hunter was just too good. He could do a better job for the animals. She regretted signing up to be a shelter scribe.

"His profiles are better than mine," Lety said.

"No es verdad," Brisa said.

"It is true."

"Do you remember that I didn't want to do this camp?"

Lety grimaced just thinking back to how hard she had to work to convince — more like beg — Brisa that enrolling in the camp would be better than ELL summer classes. Then she had to sell the idea to Brisa's family and her own family, who had to pay two hundred dollars for them both to be there. For Brisa's family, two hundred dollars wasn't that much because her father was an engineer for one of the biggest firms in town, but for Lety's family . . . it was a lot of money. Especially when ELL summer camp was free. "I only joined because of you," Brisa said. "If you start to doubt, I will doubt."

"It's tougher than I thought," Lety said.

"Tough?" Brisa said, narrowing her eyes at Lety. "Tougher than leaving your grandparents and cousins to come here? Or do you mean tough like not being invited to birthday parties with amazing cupcakes and extra-cheesy pizza that everyone talks about the next day in class?"

And just like that, a light went on in Lety's head. She felt ashamed to be making excuses. If anyone knew tough, it was definitely her and Brisa.

"Focus on those sweet puppies and precious *gatitos*. Be their voice."

"How . . ." Lety started when suddenly Brisa interrupted her with high-pitched meows.

"Meow, meow, please find me a home. Meow, meow, I don't want to stay in the shelter forever. Meow write for me —"

"Brisa!" Lety laughed. "*¡Ya!* Stop already." Brisa gave her a satisfied smile. Lety knew that with Brisa around, complaining did no good. "I will finish Bella's profile today. Then I'll write for the cats. You can help me with those."

"*¡Sí, por supuesto!* I can tell you anything you want to know about Bandit and Lorca. Bandit is a tornado with whiskers. Lorca thinks he is a lion. Hunter could never write about them, but you can. *Nos vemos, amiga*." Brisa walked off and then stopped and turned to face Lety again.

"Lety, I just realized I don't remember how to say 'give up' in Spanish anymore. Do you?"

Lety scanned her brain. She panicked, letting out a gasp.

"I don't remember it, Brisa."

"Let's keep it that way!"

Brisa swaggered down the hallway toward the cat room, leaving Lety feeling like she'd been lifted up by a strong cool wind.

Chapter 10

Colossally Perfect

"This little one was lost and found," Dr. V. said, speaking over the noisy dogs in the small-dog room. He handed Bella to Lety. "No one claimed her."

Lety wrapped the Pomeranian in her arms. How could no one come looking for her?

Daisy, the shelter manager, gave Bella a good scratch behind the ears. "And she didn't have a microchip so, sadly, no way to locate her family," Daisy said. "Can you imagine losing this love bug and never looking for her? Who would do that?"

"I don't know," Lety said as Bella licked her chin and neck nonstop. "Is there anything else I should mention in her profile? Anything other than she's a little love bug that likes to kiss?"

"The thing about Pomeranians is that they're typically no more than five pounds, but they have supersized personalities," Dr. V. answered. "Bella is probably offended that we've put her in the small-dog room because in her head she's as big as a Great Dane. Whoever adopts her needs to be on their toes."

"On their toes," Lety repeated, uncertain about what he meant. "You mean like super fast?"

"More like active and alert," Dr. Villalobos said.

"Oh yes! Perfect! Got it. Big personality and active." Lety thought of the five words she had to include in the profiles. "Would you say that Bella has a colossal personality?"

"Colossal?" Dr. V. raised his eyebrows in surprise.

"That's a big word," Daisy said to Lety with a wink.

Lety giggled because *colossal* meant massively big.

"Sure," Dr. V. said finally. "Colossal is accurate."

"Thank you, Dr. V. I think I have enough to finish her profile."

"I can't wait to see it," Dr. V. said. "It's not every day that 'colossal' shows up in an animal profile. I don't think I've ever seen that."

"I can't say I have either," Daisy said, adjusting her black-rimmed glasses onto her nose and directing her green eyes onto Lety like two spotlights.

"I'm trying to expand my vocabulary over the summer," Lety said. She felt a quick pang of worry that maybe she'd said too much, asking Dr. V. about the word *colossal*. If they found out about the contest between her and Hunter, would they kick them out? Would she lose her chance to adopt Spike? Lety handed Bella back to Dr. Villalobos.

"How is Spike doing with his foster family?"

"So far so good is what I'm hearing," Dr. Villalobos answered.

"Will he return to the shelter?"

"Oh yeah. The foster family is temporary. I want to find a family for him that won't give up on him, not just someone who wants him because he was on the news. You know what I mean?"

Lety's heart jumped at the thought that Spike might be back at the shelter soon.

"That's smart," Lety said. "So anyone can adopt him when he's back at the shelter?"

"Well, not just anyone," Dr. V. answered. "They will have to meet my strict qualifications."

Lety felt panic tighten around her. She searched his face for some sign that he was joking like he often did. Strict qualifications?

Daisy snorted, and Dr. V. finally broke into a smile. "What? I'm being totally serious. I've failed Spike so many times, sending him home with people who turned around and brought him back."

"It's not your fault," Lety said.

"You tell him, Lety." Daisy smiled. "He's too hard on himself."

"This time, I won't send Spike home with just anyone," Dr. Villalobos continued. "His next forever family will have to prove themselves to me."

"How?" Lety asked.

"Good question," Daisy said, shaking her head at Dr. V. "How?"

"I'll just know," Dr. V. said. "In my head and heart, I'll know."

Lety nodded, convinced she knew what she had to do. She had to write the best profiles to prove herself to Dr. V. She said a quick good-bye and darted out of the room toward the multipurpose room. As the cat heroes sat at a table making feather toys, she revised Bella's profile to include *colossal* and cleaned up some misspellings and run-on sentences.

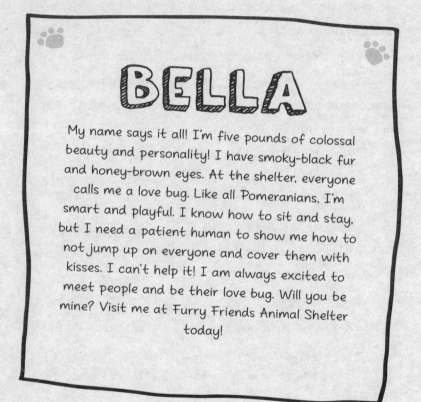

BELLA

My name says it all! I'm five pounds of colossal beauty and personality! I have smoky-black fur and honey-brown eyes. At the shelter, everyone calls me a love bug. Like all Pomeranians, I'm smart and playful. I know how to sit and stay, but I need a patient human to show me how to not jump up on everyone and cover them with kisses. I can't help it! I am always excited to meet people and be their love bug. Will you be mine? Visit me at Furry Friends Animal Shelter today!

Once she'd submitted it, Lety headed to the cat room to start profiles on Bandit, Lorca, and Chicharito. As she passed through the reception area, she spotted Alma speaking to a family at a high-top table and guiding them through adoption papers. Soon, another volunteer came out with Sawyer on a leash. The family rushed to pet him.

Sawyer was being adopted! Hunter immediately came to Lety's mind. She had to find him and let him know. She rushed to the cat room, where she had heard that Hunter was finishing his profile on Messi, a brown Siamese. She spotted him right away holding the cat on his lap, petting him to sleep.

"Hunter! Sawyer is being adopted," Lety said.

Hunter's face went pale and twisted into a frown, but he didn't move. He gazed down at Messi, who was taking a good stretch across Hunter's lap.

"I thought you'd would want to see him before he goes."

Hunter looked up.

"It's not a big deal," he said with a shrug. "All it means is that I'm winning the contest now. One down. Four more to go."

Lety stepped back in shock. Was this really just a contest to him? Didn't he care about the animals? She knew he did because he had told her about Gunner.

"But you . . ." Lety stammered. "I just thought that because he reminded you of Gunner that you'd want to . . ." Lety stopped talking when Hunter shrugged again. She was embarrassed that she had tried to be nice to Hunter. What was wrong with him? How could he think of the contest when he should be rushing out to kiss Sawyer good-bye? "Never mind."

Brisa and Kennedy came over and stood next to her.

"What's going on?" Kennedy asked.

"Sawyer is being adopted," Lety answered. "The family is leaving with him right now."

"Let's go give him a good-bye kiss," Brisa said, taking Lety's hand.

The girls joined Dr. V. outside the shelter as the family put Sawyer into a large kennel cage in the back of their SUV. Sawyer's tail wagged as he barked excitedly.

As the family backed out of the parking lot, Dr. V. and the three girls waved.

"You girls ever heard of a band named the Beatles?" Dr. V. asked.

One of the other volunteers commented that the girls were too young to know them. Dr. V. covered his face and laughed.

"I guess! I'm showing my age. Anyway, the Beatles had this song about how money can't buy you love," Dr. Villalobos explained. "And whenever I hear it, I think to myself that those guys must have never paid an adoption fee."

The girls laughed.

"Those folks just bought seventy pounds of the truest form of unconditional love known to humankind. That's what I'm saying."

"How does the song go?" Brisa asked. Dr. V. and the volunteer started singing the song as they strolled through the parking lot back toward the shelter. Brisa clapped her hands along with Dr. V. and tried to pick out the lyrics and sing along.

Kennedy sang and danced around, too, until she nudged Lety with her elbow.

"Look who's gloating over his win," Kennedy said.

Lety looked over to where Kennedy pointed and saw Hunter peering out from behind the window blinds in the shelter reception. Lety was confused. Why hadn't he come outside to kiss Sawyer good-bye? She followed Hunter's gloomy gaze toward the SUV that carried Sawyer away. It wasn't the smug look of someone winning a stupid contest. It was a look of regret.

CHAPTER 11

Two Cats Away from Victory

Hunter was winning. Outside on the deck of Kennedy's home, the girls checked the shelter's website. Once a dog or cat was adopted, the website coordinator marked the furry friend's picture with the word ADOPTED plus double exclamation points. It would stay that way for a couple of days before the website coordinator removed the profiles entirely from the website. Sawyer and Kenzie's profiles were both tagged with a bold ADOPTED!!

"Kenzie!" Lety exclaimed in joy. "Someone finally stopped at her cage. I'm so happy."

"Yay!" Brisa added.

Kennedy refreshed the page, hoping Bella or Finn would be marked as adopted, too. When their statuses didn't change, Kennedy tapped on Scout's profile.

"I have to give it to him, Hunter has a way with words," Kennedy admitted. The three girls huddled around the iPad to read Scout's profile.

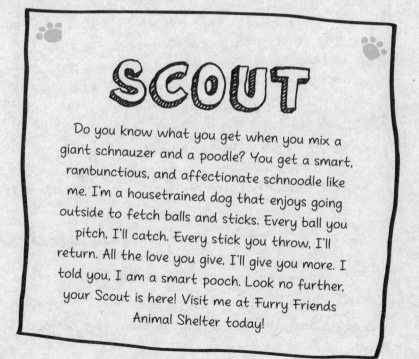

SCOUT

Do you know what you get when you mix a giant schnauzer and a poodle? You get a smart, rambunctious, and affectionate schnoodle like me. I'm a housetrained dog that enjoys going outside to fetch balls and sticks. Every ball you pitch, I'll catch. Every stick you throw, I'll return. All the love you give, I'll give you more. I told you, I am a smart pooch. Look no further, your Scout is here! Visit me at Furry Friends Animal Shelter today!

"He nailed it," Brisa said. "Has he used 'scrumptious' yet?"

"Yep," Kennedy said. With a few taps, she opened Messi's profile. Above it was an adorable image of the skinny chocolate-brown Siamese cat tangled up in blue yarn.

MESSI

Is it a comet? Is it lightning? No, it's just me, Messi, brightening up your life with my super feline speed and Siamese charms. I'm as swift as a cheetah with a ball of yarn between my soft brown paws and I'm up to date on all of my cat shots. After a long day of playing around, I enjoy a scrumptious meal and a good stretch. Can I be part of your winning team? Visit me at Furry Friends Animal Shelter today!

"Scrumptious was too easy for him," Brisa said. "I wish I had given him a bigger word."

"He still hasn't written Brooks's profile, so you can catch

up this weekend, Lety," Kennedy said. "How are the profiles going for Lorca, Bandit, and Chicharito?"

Lety pulled her notebook from her book bag.

"I have notes about Bandit, but I need more information for Chicharito's profile."

"Aw, Chicharito! The tabby with the beautiful brown eyes," Brisa squealed. "He is an angel."

"Angel?" Kennedy asked in disbelief. "That little rascal shredded all the newspaper in his cage and then destroyed the feather toys we made for him and his sisters."

"Noted! Chicharito is a four-legged monster," Lety wrote down with a smirk. "Anything else?"

"He's neutered," Kennedy said.

"He has all of his shots," Brisa added.

"Anything special-special?"

The girls gave her a blank look.

"I got nothing," Kennedy said. "He's a cat. He sleeps, purrs, licks his paws, and then will suddenly attack your feet for no good reason."

"I got something!" Brisa said. "He is named for a soccer player. Dr. Villalobos loves soccer like me."

"Okay, that helps. All I have to do is find a way to use 'infectious,' 'fusion,' or 'supersonic' now," Lety dropped her pen down on the table. "Any other impossible tasks I can add to my list today?"

Kennedy suddenly gasped and dropped her head into her hands.

"Scout's been adopted," she announced. "Hunter is now two cats away from victory."

Brisa and Lety leaned in to see Scout's profile marked ADOPTED!!

"Oh no," Brisa said softly. "But it's good for Scout."

"Yes, but bad for Lety," Kennedy said. "She's way behind."

Lety frowned at Kennedy's words. She started school "way behind" in everything: English, math, science, but she had caught up with everyone. She didn't read and write at a high school level like Hunter, but she studied hard, made good grades. Mrs. Camacho had even told her that she could opt out of ELL permanently for middle school next year, but Lety wasn't so sure if she was ready. As if reading her mind, Brisa spoke up for her.

"She can catch up."

Kennedy nodded. "I know. I'm not trying to be mean, Lety. I'd just hate it if you lost. I don't want you to spend the rest of summer camp working in the pantry. Your hair will stink like pet food."

Brisa let out a loud cackle. "You will be very popular with all the dogs at the shelter."

"I'm only interested in one dog. My sweet Spikey."

"Then show Dr. Villalobos you're the best shelter scribe," Kennedy said.

"I won't let Spike down." Lety smiled, although she felt like she could pass out from panic. Why did she ever agree to this stupid contest? There was too much at stake! She could lose and end up with smelly pet-food hair. Hunter would be proven right. Her English wasn't good enough for her to be a shelter scribe. Then there was also the risk that Dr. Villalobos would find out about the contest and decide that she wasn't fit to be Spike's forever family. She really wanted that dog.

"I got this," Lety said. *Fusion* meant the mixing of two or more things. In this case, Chicharito was a mix of pure trouble and playful cuteness. She picked up her pen and flipped to a blank page in her notebook. She knew exactly how to use *fusion* in Chicharito's profile.

ChAPTER 12

Bella on Hold

On Tuesday morning, just as Brisa and Lety arrived at the shelter, Mario wasted no time in making sure that they knew that Hunter was only two cats away from winning.

Both of Hunter's profiles for Messi, the brown Siamese, and Brooks, the black-and-white tuxedo cat, were posted on the website and, according to Mario, both were receiving lots of clicks.

"Bad news for you is that Finn's profile had to be removed. Tough luck! Sorry!"

"What? Why?" Lety asked, putting her book bag down on a table in the multipurpose room.

"Who took it down?" Brisa said, crossing her arms over her chest. She switched to Spanish, which she knew Mario understood since his grandparents were originally from Guanajuato, Mexico. *"¿Lo hiciste tú?"*

"I didn't do it," Mario said, with his hands up. "I don't have that kind of power. Geesh! Talk to Dr. V. And one more thing: That little dog that kisses everyone is on hold." Lety scrunched her eyebrows at him. Was he talking about Bella? "That means she's reserved for a family. She's practically adopted. They just have to pick her up."

"Wow, Lety!" Brisa exclaimed. "That was fast!"

The news made Lety happy, but she was stuck on what Mario had said about Finn.

"I have to talk to Dr. Villalobos," Lety said to Brisa. She rushed off and found him in the clinic. He was stocking medicines and talking to three cats who'd just been neutered or spayed and were wrapped up tight in towels like little cat burritos.

"I really liked Finn's profile and we got a few calls about him this weekend, but his issue with hats concerns me," Dr. V. explained to Lety.

"People wanted to adopt him?"

Dr. V. nodded. "They were interested, but I didn't feel right sending him home with a family until I've fully addressed his behavioral issues."

Lety nodded. She understood. However, without Finn, she was short one profile. This meant there was no way to beat Hunter and win the contest. The most she could hope for was a 4–4 tie at the end of the week.

"I'm sorry, Lety. Are you upset?"

"Me? No," she said, not realizing she had been frowning. She forced a smile. "I only want him to find a forever family."

"Me, too," Dr. V. said. "I know you're putting a lot of time into writing the profiles, so I wanted you to know that was the only reason for taking Finn's profile down."

"I understand," Lety said. "Is there maybe another dog I could write about?"

"I'm sure there is, but let me give it some thought. You know, you and Hunter are writing some phenomenal profiles."

"Thanks."

"Hunter wrote a profile . . . I forget which one it was, but he used 'beckon,' and then in another one he used 'rambunctious'?" He shook his head in amazement. "Totally blew my mind."

"He writes at a high school level."

"And you," he continued. He grabbed a flyer from the top of his desk. "This Chicharito profile is like a professional advertisement."

"Really?"

Dr. Villalobos read the profile out loud, making Lety squirm. Was he onto the contest?

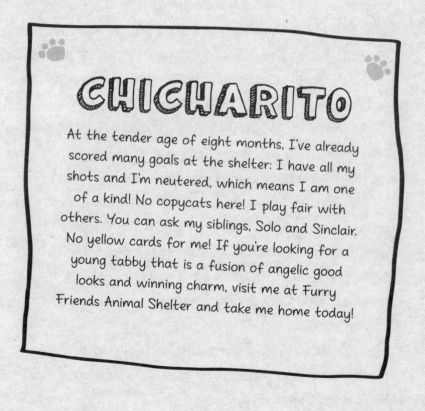

CHICHARITO

At the tender age of eight months, I've already scored many goals at the shelter: I have all my shots and I'm neutered, which means I am one of a kind! No copycats here! I play fair with others. You can ask my siblings, Solo and Sinclair. No yellow cards for me! If you're looking for a young tabby that is a fusion of angelic good looks and winning charm, visit me at Furry Friends Animal Shelter and take me home today!

"Fusion?" Dr. V. said. "Angelic?"

Lety felt suddenly warm all over, like she was the one wrapped up tight in a towel.

"Then today, Hunter submitted a profile for Brooks using the word 'cerise'!" Dr. V. continued. "I had to google it. Have you ever heard that word?"

Lety was certain that her face was flushed cerise at that very moment. Dr. Villalobos was onto them. She was certain of it! Still, she couldn't deny that she knew the word.

"It is a deep pink color," Lety said. "It is very popular. People use it for an accent wall in the dining room or master bedroom. At least that is what my mom says."

"Accent wall, you say?" Dr. V. said, arching his eyebrows. "Your mom must be a home designer?"

"She paints homes and apartments," Lety answered.

"Did you teach Hunter that word? I mean, doesn't it seem strange that he knows it?" Dr. V. said, which made Lety nervous. She could almost see the pieces in Dr. V.'s head coming together. She wished that one of the cat burritos would wake up, but they were as still and quiet as the air closing in on her.

"Hunter and I hardly even talk," Lety answered. She desperately wanted to change the subject. "Dr. Villalobos, how's Spike doing? Will he back soon?"

"He'll be back —" Dr. V. said, when his phone pinged. He pulled it from his jeans pocket. Lety was grateful for the distraction. She'd thought she was done for. Somehow he knew about the contest. Or maybe he didn't, but he was definitely suspicious of all the words they were using. "Bella's forever family is here," he said, looking up from his phone. "Let's go see the little love bug off."

Lety let out a big sigh of relief. For now, Bella had saved her, but she had to warn Hunter. Dr. V. was definitely onto them!

CHAPTER 13

All That Matters

Lety found Hunter in the multipurpose room, writing in his notebook. As she stepped behind him, she peeked over his shoulder and saw that he wasn't writing at all. He was sketching a dog. The dog looked a lot like Sawyer, but she knew it must be his dog, Gunner. She had planned to warn him about Dr. V. asking about the big words they were using but instead left him alone with his sketch. She took a seat next to Brisa and Kennedy as the guest speaker turned on the computer and projector.

"The score is three to one now," Kennedy said, flashing a thumbs-up at Lety. "Congrats on Bella!"

Lety smiled, pleased with herself, but then she remembered about Finn. Kennedy didn't know yet that Finn had been removed from the website and was no longer adoptable. She would have to tell her later, since the guest speaker was starting.

The speaker's name was Zoe. She was part of a program called the Rescue Team. She clicked through a slide show of photographs that showed members of the Rescue Team saving chained-up dogs from the cold and delivering pet food to families that had "limited financial resources." Lety knew that "limited financial resources" meant families like hers.

"We work closely with the folks in the pantry. They prepare bags of pet food and we deliver them every month to families who need them."

"If they can't afford food for their pets, why do they have them?" one of the girls asked. Zoe was just about to answer when Hunter cut her off.

"Because they love them, Jenna. Duh!" Hunter said. "Just because they don't have money doesn't mean they don't have hearts."

"Chill out, Hunter." Kennedy sighed. "Sheesh! She was just asking a question."

"A stupid question," Hunter mumbled.

"You're stupid," Jenna snapped. "I wasn't saying they didn't have hearts."

"Okay, there are no stupid questions," Zoe said, rushing in to control the discussion, but Jenna, Kennedy, and Hunter were still mouthing off at one another. "And no one is stupid, okay?" Zoe said, raising her voice to get the three of them to stop. Lety felt sorry for Zoe and sat up straight to show she was paying attention. Brisa followed Lety's example. Once the bickering back and forth stopped, Zoe started again.

"Sometimes people's lives change," Zoe continued. Lety looked at Hunter. He had pulled his cap down over his eyes and was staring at his sketch. "People lose their jobs, divorce, or get sick, and all of sudden they struggle to feed their families, including their pets. Our Rescue Team helps identify these families. We supply them with food and access to veterinary care until the family is back on their feet. It's rewarding to lend this type of support to our community."

Zoe scanned the room, as if checking to see if she had put out the fire. Jenna pouted. Hunter dipped down farther into his chair and under his baseball cap.

Lety was unsure if now was a time to speak, but she wanted to thank Zoe. She'd always felt that the most important words she'd learned in English were *thank you*. Mrs. Camacho always said that you could tell a lot about a person by what words they want to learn in another language. In the third grade, Lety remembered a group of fifth-grade girls stopping her after recess and asking her how to say "ugly pig" and "go away" in Spanish. It was the only time that these girls had ever spoken to her. On the spot, Lety had decided instead to tell them that "ugly pig" was *guapa* and "go away" was *sale bien*. As they walked away and repeated the new Spanish words back and forth to one another, Lety wondered why they didn't want to learn nice Spanish words or expressions. If they only wanted to say mean things in Spanish, then what did that say about their character or how they felt about Spanish speakers like her? By teaching them nice words, Lety felt like she had achieved a small victory.

Zoe called on Lety.

"Thank you for helping the families keep their pets," Lety said.

"You're welcome," she said with a smile.

Lety wanted to say more. She wanted to tell her thank you for helping out families who were poor in cash, but not poor in love. She wanted to tell Zoe and the entire room that if her family had a dog, it would be the most loved animal in the world. Her father, she knew, would feed the dog before he fed himself. That's how he was in Mexico with all the strays that roamed the streets. Her mom also loved animals. In Mexico, her paintings of stray dogs and cats were always bestsellers among European tourists. When she sold one, she gave the strays a tasty treat of a tamale or taco. Lety wanted to say all of this but hesitated, frozen silent by her doubts about whether she could express it correctly in front of the whole room.

"We don't want money to be a reason for a family to give up their pet," Zoe said. "That solves nothing."

"That's right," Lety said, surprising herself. Brisa and Kennedy snorted and giggled at her outburst.

"As long as you love them, that's all that matters," Hunter muttered from under his hat. A wave of shocked murmurs spread throughout the entire room. Was Hunter talking about love? Brisa passed Lety a look of pure shock.

"Mr. Shruggy Llama has a *corazón*," she whispered. Lety wasn't shocked that Hunter had a heart. She had witnessed him talking about his dog, Gunner. She had heard his soft voice. She peered over at Hunter, and when she did, he caught her glance and smiled.

ChaPTeR 14

Don't Make Eye Contact

"Ready to swoon?" Lety asked Kennedy and Brisa. Bandit's profile was pinned up on the bulletin board in the reception area where the girls waited for their rides home.

BANDIT

Ready to swoon? I'm a domestic short hair with coal-black fur and sapphire-blue eyes. My favorite activities are chasing feathers, playing with balls of yarn, and rolling around in newspaper. I used to live in a home, so I know how to use a litter box. My former family said that the only reason they had to give me up was because everyone was sneezing. I hope I don't make you achoo! Like a true bandit, I will steal your heart with my infectious purring. Visit me at Furry Friends Animal Shelter and take me home today!

"Nice use of 'infectious,'" Kennedy added. "How's Lorca's profile? Are you done with it?"

"Almost," Lety said. Kennedy seemed happy with that and waved good-bye as she rushed out to her mom's car. Normally, the girls would go over to Kennedy's house to swim, but Brisa's mom was picking them up today and taking them to the grocery store. She was six months pregnant and craving a special Bolivian dish called *picante de pollo*.

She wanted to make it for lunch. As Lety watched Kennedy jump into her mom's white SUV, she spotted Hunter outside alone. He shifted from foot to foot, kept his head down and his hands tucked into his jeans pockets. She hoped Brisa's mom would show up soon so that she could say bye to Hunter as they left, but as soon as she wished it, a tan car drove up.

"Sorry I'm late, Hunter," the woman called out from behind the wheel. Lety moved closer to the window to watch. Two little boys were in the backseat.

"It's okay, Grandma," Hunter said, opening the passenger door. He was about to take a seat when she yelled out again.

"Oh, Hunter! I left the gas thing open again."

"I got it." Hunter exited the car to shut the gas cap. "It's all set." Lety watched as he got into the front passenger seat and his grandma grabbed his face and gave him a kiss on the cheek.

"Thank you, baby," she said. Just then, Brisa's mother arrived, pulling up behind Hunter's grandma's car.

Lety and Brisa quickly rushed out as the tan car drove away.

"Surprise!" Eddie shouted as the girls got into the car. "Are you surprised to see me?"

Lety shook her head. "No, I knew you were coming. I heard Mom on the phone with Mrs. Quispe this morning."

"I wasn't surprised either, Eduardo," Brisa said with a wink. "Did you see Mrs. Camacho today?"

"I see her every day. She brought her guitar."

"You guys sang today? What songs?"

"We sang 'This Land Is Your Land,' and a song called 'Beautiful.'"

"I want to sing songs," Brisa said with a pout. "You're so lucky."

"I know," Eddie quipped.

"But you get to play with cats, Brisa," Lety said. "That's fun."

"You're right, but I miss Mrs. Camacho and her guitar. Sing me 'Beautiful,' Eduardo. *¡Por favor!*"

"Okay," Eddie said before starting up the first verse in his small voice. After a few verses, Brisa's mom smiled at him through the rearview mirror.

"Tienes la voz de un ángel," she said. Eddie blushed but continued singing. Lety was amazed at her fearless brother, who was happy to sing sappy songs about being beautiful.

At the grocery store, while Brisa and her mom stopped at the pharmacy counter, Eddie and Lety looked at magazines in a nearby aisle. Eddie had just grabbed a magazine filled with word searches and crossword puzzles when a loud man's voice made them jump. It was as if the voice was right behind them. Lety and Eddie looked around, but the angry voice was coming from somewhere else. That's when it hit Lety that the voice was coming from the pharmacy area where Brisa and Mrs. Quispe were.

"You're in America!" the man's harsh voice roared again. Lety peeked around the aisle toward the pharmacy. From the edge of the aisle, she saw a man in a red baseball cap, yelling behind Brisa and Brisa's mom. Eddie peeked, too.

"Who is he yelling at, Lety?"

"I don't know," Lety said. She stepped out of the aisle. The man was hovering too close behind Brisa and her mom at the pharmacy counter. Their backs were to him as he yelled over them toward the pharmacist. Lety didn't like the way it looked. She took a few steps closer but stopped once Brisa met her gaze. Brisa shook her head slowly at Lety in warning, as if saying "Stay where you are." Lety stopped in her tracks.

"Sir! You cannot yell at them that way. You need to —" said a woman's voice from behind the pharmacy counter.

"I'm speaking to you, too. You need to speak English," the man said. "Why are you helping them in Spanish? This is America. You're just encouraging them."

Lety hated the way he said "encouraging them." He spit the words out of his mouth like something that tasted bad.

"Sir! I'm going to have to call my manager if you don't stop this," the woman said. Brisa's mom dabbed her eyes with a tissue. Brisa took her mom's hand, but they stood and remained there as the man hovered behind them. Lety's mind shot back to what Dr. Villalobos had told them about aggressive dogs. Be stiff. Rigid. Don't make eye contact. She stared down at the eggshell-white tiled floor with the smoky-gray swirls. Eddie clutched Lety's arm with moist hands.

"Why is he yelling?" Eddie asked.

"I don't know," Lety said. "He's mad."

"About what?"

Lety shushed her little brother. "Don't make eye contact with him."

"If you don't know English, learn it or go back to Mexico where you came from," the man continued.

Eddie suddenly raced toward the man.

"You can't talk to my friends like that!" Eddie yelled. "They're from Bolivia. Not Mexico. And they're learning English like me."

"Eddie!" Lety yelled, going after her brother. Eddie wedged himself between the man and Brisa's mom, but Lety quickly pulled him out and wrapped her arms around his small frame. She looked at the man and got a good view of his red-freckled face and brown hair. The man paused and looked over Eddie and Lety. She felt her brother trembling in her arms and it made her angry. The man wouldn't hurt them, would he? They were in a grocery store filled with hundreds of other people. They were safe, right? Didn't he see Brisa's mom was pregnant? She was filling a doctor's prescription. Why was he picking on them?

"Tell him, Lety," Eddie said, crinkling his brows at the man.

Brisa finally turned toward the red-faced man but looked too frightened to say anything. Brisa's mom was crying now, and the woman behind the counter was trying to comfort her.

"Leave us alone," Lety said, shoving the words out as straight as she could so they didn't sound shaky.

The man took a step back and scoffed.

"Sir! I'm going to have to ask you to leave," said another man, who was dressed in a shirt and tie. His name tag read STORE MANAGER. Lety's shoulders dropped in relief. Eddie wriggled in her arms, and she realized that she'd been holding him too tight. She loosened her grip around him, but he stayed snug, not moving an inch.

"You tell your employees to stop speaking Spanish. This is America. See if I shop here at your store again."

"That's probably best, sir. We appreciate your past business," the manager said, walking behind the man down the aisle and out the store exit.

It was all over. Lety felt light-headed, like the time a soccer ball had smacked her on the side of the head. Mrs. Quispe grabbed all of them close to her and bawled softly as the woman behind the counter offered gentle apologies. A few people wandered by and gave them sympathetic glances.

"That man was mean, Lety!" Eddie cried, turning to her and wrapping his skinny arms around her waist. "Why was he like that?"

Lety held her brother close. "I don't know, but he's gone now."

CHAPTER 15

Deep Blue Dreams

Over the dinner table at Lety's house, Mrs. Quispe explained everything to Lety's parents. Eddie sat on his dad's lap, burying his face against his neck.

"I tried to make him stop, Dad," Eddie blurted out every so often. "He was mean."

Lety sat on the couch with Brisa in silence, listening to their parents going back and forth, trying to understand why the man was so angry. Lety's father shared a story about a time he was at a bank. A man accused him of jumping the line in front of him, although he hadn't, and called him all sorts of names. Her father watched his words, knowing Lety, Brisa, and Eddie were listening. He rarely talked about his time alone in the US. He always reassured Lety that people were nice here. He never complained. Now he was sharing a bad story. Eddie looked up, horrified.

"When did that happen, Papá?" Eddie asked.

"*No te preocupes, mijo.*"

"I want to know," Eddie continued.

Lety's father said that the man yelled at him to get out of the country. Lety's father didn't know how to defend himself in English. No one else spoke up for him. He was embarrassed and left without cashing his check.

Brisa shook her head slowly.

"I'm not returning to the shelter," she said softly to Lety.

"What? *¿Por qué no?*"

"I have to improve my English, not make cat toys."

"But you love the cats," Lety said.

A tear trickled down Brisa's cheek. "It's true. Especially Bandit, Chicharito, Wilde, Lorca, Messi, Solo, and Sinclair. All of them, but it doesn't help me. I have to be able to speak English like Eddie."

"But, Brisa . . ."

Brisa shook her head.

"You speak like Eddie."

"No, I don't. I wanted to say something . . . something to that man, but my mind went empty."

"That's because you were afraid. We were afraid, too."

"Eddie could still speak in English. You, too," Brisa said.

"Please come back to the shelter with me," Lety said. "It won't be the same without you. Plus, you said we shouldn't give up. We are tough."

"I'm not. No more. English will make me tough. You, too. Come to ELL class. You are my desk buddy, remember?"

"My parents paid a lot for me to be there," Lety said. "Plus, I'm a shelter scribe."

"Then stay there. I've made up my mind," Brisa said. The way she said it, Lety knew it was true and there was nothing more she could say.

Lety swallowed hard. She didn't want to be away from Brisa, but she couldn't leave the shelter now. The choice between the shelter and being with Brisa was like someone pulling her heart apart. She wondered if this is what Dr. Villalobos meant by hurting "like the dickens."

"I'm going to just show up to Mrs. Camacho's class. I hope she doesn't mind."

Lety shook her head. She knew Mrs. Camacho wouldn't mind having Brisa back this summer.

"She'll be happy, Brisa," Lety said. "You're one of her best students."

"The thing is, I was starting to feel like I belonged here. Being at the shelter with all the other campers, making toys for the *gatitos*, and . . . now I just want to be back with my *abuela*. I miss her more than ever. I want to be back in La Paz. This place will never feel like home."

"It will, Brisa," Lety said.

"How can you be sure?"

"Because we're here together."

Brisa took Lety's hand and held it. Lety hoped she'd never let go, but deep down she could feel her best friend slipping away.

Later that night in bed, Lety couldn't sleep. She was upset that Brisa wasn't returning to the shelter. Across the room from her, Eddie wriggled around in his twin bed and let out a few whimpers like the kittens at the shelter when they were afraid. When Eddie's whimpers turned into an all-out sob, her father came in and switched on the light.

"Mijo," her dad whispered. He sat at the edge of Eddie's bed and pulled the covers to see Eddie's wet, teary face. *"¿Mijo, por qué lloras?"*

"I don't want people to yell at me."

Lety's father wiped Eddie's tears away with his calloused fingers.

"No llores, Eduardo," he said. "No cry."

Eddie's sobbing crumbled Lety's heart like chalk on the sidewalk. She was used to Eddie always being confident and positive. She imagined herself taking purple chalk and scrawling words that would make her little brother feel better. She remembered what Mrs. Camacho had said about Eddie's English being better because he was younger when he started to learn it.

"People won't yell at you, Eddie," Lety said, sitting up in bed. "You're young and your brain is a sponge. You speak English better than all of us."

"Not just me. I don't want them to yell at you, Mom, Dad, or Brisa either," Eddie cried, covering his face with his hands. "Or Mrs. Quispe. I don't want —" Eddie voice broke into a long wail. Lety helplessly looked at her father, unsure of what else to say. Then her father did something she never expected. He reached for a paint swatch from Eddie's nightstand. As Eddie sobbed, her father started reading the colors aloud.

"Dark Denim. Durango Blue. Jean Jacket Blue."

Eddie dropped his hands from his eyes and glanced up at his father. A smile crept across his face.

"Arizona Sky. Indigo Night."

"Papá!" Eddie laughed. "You pronounced all of them wrong."

"*¿Qué?* I say it correct, no?" Lety's father winked playfully at Lety.

"Noooo," Eddie said with a chuckle.

"Tomorrow, you and Lety teach me say English correct. Sleep now, *mijo*."

"Okay, but I get to be the teacher," Eddie said, flopping down against his pillow. As her father tucked Eddie back into bed, Lety wiped her tears with her bedsheets.

Her father came over, leaned down, and kissed Lety's forehead. He smelled minty, like the medicine her mom rubbed on his hands after long days of painting cabinets. She wondered if his hands or back were hurting.

Before he walked out of the room and switched off the lights, Lety called out to him.

"Papá?"

"*¿Sí, mija?*"

"Are you glad we came here?"

Her father paused at the doorway and gave her a tired smile.

"*Sí, mija.* We make dream here. Better life for you."

"Even if they don't want us here?"

"*Sí, mija.* No one can stop dreams. *Buenas noches, mi vida.*"

"*Buenas noches,* Papá."

He turned off the light, filling the room with darkness except for a ray of light that streamed under the door into the room. It created a blue haze on the floor between the two beds. Lety studied the blue glow. It reminded her of the deep end of a swimming pool.

As if it was another color on a paint swatch, Lety named it.

"*Sueños azules oscuros,*" she whispered. Deep Blue Dreams. As she dozed off to sleep, she, Brisa, Eddie, and her entire family dove into the blue sea. They splashed around, free of doubt, free to speak whichever language they wanted, and even when her feet couldn't touch the bottom, she wasn't afraid.

ChaPTeR 16

Good News, Bad News

Walking through the front door of the shelter without Brisa was lonelier and stranger than Lety expected. All night she kept hoping Brisa would change her mind, but a phone call from Brisa's mom in the morning confirmed it: Brisa was going to ELL class for the rest of the summer. Lety's stomach flip-flopped at the thought of a full day without Brisa.

Kennedy and Mario raced up to Lety, eager to tell her the latest on the contest.

"Best day ever!" Kennedy began. Lety wasn't so sure. So far, the day had felt rough. "Messi and Chicharito were adopted last night by one of the coaches for the city's soccer team."

"Check it out," Mario said, shoving his cell phone in front of Lety. "He's already posted pictures online." He scrolled to a photo of the coach and his family with the two cats. It was captioned: "Goal! Our family is complete."

Lety looked back and forth from the picture to Kennedy and Mario. As they carried on excitedly, Lety had a feeling that the contest was more important to them than to her and Hunter.

"The score is four to two now," Kennedy said. "You're definitely catching up."

"Catching up? She's down by three pets. Hunter is one adoption from winning it all," Mario said. "Looks like you'll be scooping dog food soon, Lety."

Kennedy nudged him hard, sending him away rubbing his ribs.

"It's not over until the fat lady sings," Kennedy hollered at him.

"Who is the fat lady?" Lety asked. "I don't think we're supposed to say 'fat.'"

"It's just a silly expression," Kennedy said, and then looked around. "Wait a minute, where's Brisa?"

"She's not coming," Lety answered. "She's decided to go to summer school."

"What? Why? We're making tuna pops for the cats today."

Lety wasn't sure if she should tell Kennedy about what happened at the store. Dredging it up meant having to think about her brother crying, Mrs. Quispe crying, and repeating the man's awful words.

"I don't understand," Kennedy said. "She was looking forward to making tuna pops. Did she say why? Should I text her?"

Lety shook her head. "Nothing will change her mind."

"What happened, Lety?"

Kennedy wasn't going to give up until she knew the reason Brisa wasn't there, so Lety pulled her by the hand over to the washer and dryer room. She told Kennedy the whole story.

"He kept telling us that we were in America and should speak English."

"What a bully," Kennedy hissed. "Did you ask him which America he meant? South America or North America? Because Brisa's family is from South America and Mexico is part of North America. So what did he mean that this was

America and everyone should speak English? Did you ask him that?"

"He didn't give us a chance to say anything. He just yelled," Lety said. "Eddie was so upset. He could barely sleep last night."

"Oh no!" Kennedy shook her head furiously. "Poor Eddie! I'd like to slug this bully."

Lety smiled at the thought of Kennedy going after the man.

"I mean, I'd really like to smack him right in the snout and say, 'Hey, big guy, learn your continents! And *cállate la boca*!' "

Lety burst out laughing as Kennedy practiced her rough Spanish and got worked up.

"I mean it, Lety."

"I believe you."

"What a bully!"

"*Tranquila,* Kennedy." Lety hugged Kennedy. "Don't go and turn crazy poodle on me."

Kennedy laughed and fanned herself as if to cool off. "What are we going to do about Brisa? She has to come back."

"I know."

"This is so horrible that I don't even want to give you more bad news," Kennedy said, covering her mouth like she was scared.

Lety closed her eyes for a second. She definitely wasn't in the mood for more bad news, but she took a deep breath. "Tell me."

Kennedy pulled her iPad from her bag. "Hunter's profile for Brooks is really popular. He used the word you gave him: 'cerise.' And it's sort of awesome. So . . ."

Lety took the iPad. At the top of the screen was a photo of Brooks the tuxedo cat peering out from behind a vase of flowers.

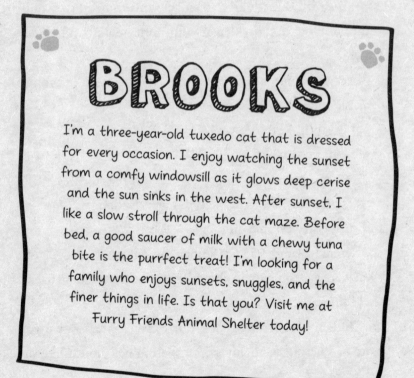

BROOKS

I'm a three-year-old tuxedo cat that is dressed for every occasion. I enjoy watching the sunset from a comfy windowsill as it glows deep cerise and the sun sinks in the west. After sunset, I like a slow stroll through the cat maze. Before bed, a good saucer of milk with a chewy tuna bite is the purrfect treat! I'm looking for a family who enjoys sunsets, snuggles, and the finer things in life. Is that you? Visit me at Furry Friends Animal Shelter today!

"It's amazing," Lety said. "He really deserves to be shelter scribe."

"You do, too," Kennedy said. "And Lorca's profile? Is it done?" Kennedy placed her hands on her hips. "You still have a chance to win this thing."

Lety pulled out her notebook.

"I'm on it," she said, and then raced to the cat room. Lety planned to write the best profile she could in honor of Eddie, Brisa, and English Language Learners everywhere!

CHAPTER 17

First Draft

Lety found Lorca lounging on the highest shelf in the cat room overlooking the cages below. His golden eyes were as large as sunflowers and flickered like glitter.

"Lorca thinks he's a lion," Kennedy said, pulling a gray kitten named Kiwi out of its cage. "Dr. Villalobos says he sits up there so he can watch all of us. I think he secretly judges us."

"How does he get up there?" Lety asked, glancing around the room to spot Lorca's path.

"He leaps and pounces from the tops of the cages. He's the only one Dr. V. allows to roam. He's wild and free like a lion in sub-Saharan Africa, but he doesn't bother anyone. He's chill," Kennedy said. "You should definitely add that to your profile."

"And his name? Do you know where it's from?"

Kennedy shook her head. "No clue."

Lety jotted a few notes and began to write what she hoped was her best profile yet.

As soon as Lety got home, she called Brisa. She wanted to know how her first day back at ELL class went and also share Lorca's profile with her.

"It's just a first draft," Lety explained to Brisa.

"Read it to me."

"'A lion? A tiger? No, I am Lorca! I am a golden fluffy cat that loves to climb, leap, and pounce! Here at the shelter, I roam, keeping an eye on the kittens in the clinic. Everyone says I am the king of the cats because I am loyal and brave. Will you join my kingdom? Visit me at Furry Friends Animal Shelter today!'"

"It is so good, Lety," Brisa said. "I like that word 'fluffy.' It's one of those English words that actually sounds like what it is. You know?"

Lety laughed. "You're right. But I still have to use 'super-sonic' in the profile and I don't know what Lorca's name means."

"I know," Brisa said. "Lorca is a poet from Spain. He lived a long, long time ago. My mom has a couple of his books at our home because she was a teacher in La Paz. She studied all the poets: José Martí, Pablo Neruda, Octavio Paz, Sor Juana Inés. All of them."

Lety stared down at Lorca's profile.

"I have to revise it."

"*¿Por qué?* It is good."

"If Lorca is named for a poet, then I'm going to write a poem. What do you think?"

"Are you going to try to rhyme 'supersonic'? Maybe 'chronic' . . . wait! Is that a real word? I don't know. I think I made it up."

"'Chronic' is a real word, Brisa." Lety chuckled. "It may not rhyme totally, but I'll try."

"Did anyone ask about me at the shelter today?" Brisa said in a voice that reminded Lety of a puppy that wanted to be held.

"Everyone."

"Did you tell them why I wasn't there?"

"I told Kennedy."

"What did she say?"

"She went all crazy poodle. She called the man a bully and then said we should have asked him what America he was talking about: South America? North America? She wants to punch him in the snout."

Lety laughed remembering Kennedy getting all worked up, but Brisa didn't react. The silence worried Lety.

"Brisa?"

"Last night, my mind was wild," she said. "I kept thinking about all of the things I wanted to say to that man. I speak two languages! He only speaks one. But both languages failed me . . ." Brisa's voice faded, then rose again like a tsunami wave. "As if we don't know that we have to learn English. What does he think we're doing? Does he think people can learn English in a day? He is ignorant. Every day, we tighten our tongues to speak English. Hide our accents. Practice sounding like everyone in class. He doesn't know what we do to learn English."

"And he never bothered to ask," Lety said.

"Exactly! He just yelled," Brisa added. "Yelled at me and my pregnant mom."

"I know," Lety said.

"I was so sleepy today that I dozed off a few times while Mrs. Camacho was reading a story." Brisa let out a nervous laugh. "She gave us homework. A book report. I haven't read a book all summer. I need to find something to read."

"I can help you, Brisa."

"Thanks, but I have to stop depending on you."

Lety felt like a harsh wind had just toppled her over onto her butt and lifted Brisa up into the air, away from her, like a cloud drifting farther and farther.

"I'm sorry, but it is because we won't always be together," Brisa said. "We won't always be desk buddies. I know that now and I have to start doing things on my own. Don't be mad. *¿Estás enojada,* Lety?"

"I'm not mad," Lety answered. She took a deep breath and wished that man had never said anything to them. What gave him the right to yell at them? Because of him, she felt a giant wall creeping up between her and Brisa. She was mad, but not at her best friend. "I'm a little sad."

"Don't be sad," she said. "Can you do me a favor and give the cats a *beso* for me?"

"All of them?"

"Yes, kiss them all!" Brisa laughed a wicked laugh. "And hurry up and beat Hunter. You deserve to be shelter scribe."

Before bed, Lety had turned Lorca's profile into a poem that was still less than a hundred words. Short and sweet. That's how Dr. Villalobos liked it.

Her family wanted to hear it.

"If you don't understand, I can translate," Eddie told them, pulling out a tablet of yellow paper. "Mrs. Camacho says I'm a good translator."

Lety stood up at the table and began to read.

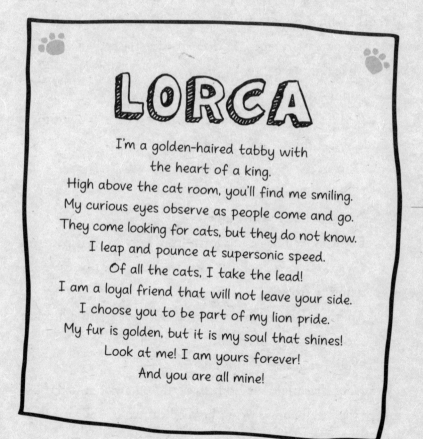

LORCA

I'm a golden-haired tabby with
the heart of a king.
High above the cat room, you'll find me smiling.
My curious eyes observe as people come and go.
They come looking for cats, but they do not know.
I leap and pounce at supersonic speed.
Of all the cats, I take the lead!
I am a loyal friend that will not leave your side.
I choose you to be part of my lion pride.
My fur is golden, but it is my soul that shines!
Look at me! I am yours forever!
And you are all mine!

Lety's mom and dad clapped wildly. Eddie stood up, grabbing for the paper.

"I want to read it! Can I read it, Lety?"

Lety passed it to him.

Eddie cleared his throat and read Lety's poem, pausing and stumbling at words he didn't know. When he reached the last line, he added a roar that made everyone laugh. As her parents hugged Eddie, an idea flashed in front of Lety like lightning.

"Eddie, did you understand all the words?"

Eddie shrugged. "Some of them. I didn't know 'supersonic,' but I think it means 'fast.'"

"Fast as the speed of sound."

"Whoa! That's the fastest."

"Do you like reading aloud?"

Eddie looked back and forth from Lety to their parents.

"We do it at school, but this was more fun because it's not a boring story."

Another flash lit up her heart. She gave her little brother a kiss on the top of his head.

"You just gave me an idea!"

Later that night, as Eddie was tucked away in bed, Lety kept the small lamp next to her bed turned on. She couldn't shake the idea that she'd had earlier. What if? she thought, letting the idea stretch out in front of her like a cat.

What if ELL students like her brother and Brisa could come to the shelter to read to the dogs and cats? The dogs needed the company. The cats would love the attention. Then Brisa could come back to the shelter. She could be with the kittens and improve her English at the same time.

Lety laid her head back against her pillow. There were only two people she needed to convince. Would Dr. Villalobos like it? Would Mrs. Camacho agree to it? Lety dozed off, certain it was worth a try.

ChAPTeR 18

Barrel of Dog Food

As soon as Lety arrived to the shelter, she typed up Lorca's profile and emailed it to Dr. Villalobos for his review. She hoped he'd like it so much that when she approached him later, he'd support her new idea.

That morning, she had practiced what she thought were her best points: Having ELL students read to the pets would help to socialize the dogs and cats. It might also bring more people to the shelter. If needed, Lety was prepared to do a demo for Dr. Villalobos and read to one of the cat burritos. She was confident she could convince him.

She was on her way to Dr. Villalobos's office when she spotted Hunter and Mario exchanging a high five in the hallway. Hunter wore a big smile and seemed happier than she'd ever seen him. It stopped her in her tracks. When Hunter saw her, his smile faded. Mario grinned from ear to ear.

"Contest is over! Hunter gets the win!" Mario shouted. Lety let her shoulders drop. She frowned and then remembered that if Hunter won, that meant Brooks, the tuxedo cat, had found a home with a family. It was awesome news, except that now she wouldn't be able to write any more profiles.

"Brooks was adopted?" she asked, and the two boys confirmed with nods.

"Yep!" Mario said. "You lost."

"But you don't have to scoop dog food in the pantry," Hunter said.

"Yes, she does." Mario turned to him, shocked. "That was the deal. She agreed."

"I know, but things have changed," Hunter said.

"What things?" Mario asked.

"Everything." Alma's voice rang out as she walked up behind Mario and Hunter with Dr. Villalobos, and Kennedy at her side. They must have heard the entire conversation.

"Did you tattle on us?" Mario said to Kennedy. She rolled her eyes. Dr. Villalobos waved off Mario's charge.

"She didn't do anything," Dr. V. said with a gentle voice. "Hunter and Lety, could you come with me to the clinic to talk?"

Lety felt hot all over. She wanted to cry, but a knot as thick as rope formed in her throat. She could barely breathe, let alone cry. Hunter looked no better. Both of them dipped their heads low as they walked behind Dr. V. toward the clinic.

Inside Dr. Villalobos's office, Spike was cuddled up on Dr. Villalobos's chair and lifted his head to bark at them as they walked in.

"Spike is back!" Lety said. She rushed to him and gave him a few kisses on his muzzle. Spike quickly returned the kisses. "Sweet boy!" Lety said. She was so happy to see Spike, she almost forgot why she was in Dr. V.'s office in the first place. Dr. V. pulled out two chairs. Spike followed her as she sat down next to Hunter in one of the chairs. Spike lay down at her feet and gnawed at one of her shoelaces until Dr. V. made him stop with a short whistle.

Dr. Villalobos leaned against the edge of his desk, stretching his long legs in front of him.

"Who wants to start and tell me about this shelter scribe contest?"

Lety started thinking of what she should say. How she should apologize. Her mind raced to process the right words in the right order, but Dr. Villalobos took her silence for not wanting to answer.

"Okay, let me tell you what I know. You two can correct me if I get anything wrong. Both of you wanted to be shelter scribes, but you didn't want to work together. Instead of going at this project to help the pets, you decided to make a contest out of it," Dr. Villalobos said. "So far so good, right?"

Lety and Hunter nodded.

"Somehow you decided that the contest would involve strange, complicated words in every profile. Words like 'rambunctious,' 'supersonic,' 'colossal,' and my favorite new word to describe sunsets: 'cerise'!" Hunter glanced at Lety in disbelief. "How am I doing? Stop me if I'm wrong."

Lety nodded.

"I'm on the right track, then," he said. "What I still haven't figured out and what Kennedy would not tell me was, what was the contest for? What does the winner get?"

Hunter shifted in his seat and looked at Lety again. "I can tell him, okay?"

Lety was relieved that he was willing to speak because the knot in her throat was not disappearing anytime soon. Then again, for a second she worried he'd blame her for everything. She wasn't sure she could totally trust him.

"The winner gets to be the only shelter scribe. The loser has to join the Food Pantry Heroes to scoop dog food into bags."

Dr. Villalobos closed his eyes and nodded as if it all made sense to him.

"Let me get this right," he started. "Our animals here at Furry Friends were just part of a contest for you both?"

He let the question float above the room. Lety wanted to pluck it from the air and tell him no. She never wanted the contest. She just wanted the chance to be shelter scribe. She loved the animals and was happy even when one of Hunter's dogs or cats were adopted.

"It was really me, sir," Hunter said. Lety couldn't believe her ears. Hunter was taking the full blame. "I didn't want to share. And I didn't think Lety could write very well. I pushed for the contest because I thought I could beat her."

"I don't understand. Why didn't you think Lety could write very well?"

Hunter shrugged. Lety knew that shrug. It wasn't an I-don't-care shrug, it was an I-don't-want-to-say-the-words-that-might-hurt-someone shrug.

"It's because at school I'm still learning English. Three years learning," Lety said.

"Really? I had no idea," Dr. V. said, his voice as tender as kitten whiskers. "Your writing is just as good as our first shelter scribe's. I've caught a few misspellings, but that's it." He turned his gaze to Hunter. "She proved you wrong. Eh, Hunter?"

Hunter nodded. "Yes, sir." Then he glanced at Lety. "I was off the mark. I'm sorry."

Lety felt like her heart would explode with joy. Hunter Farmer had just apologized to her without an adult telling him to do it. Dr. V. caught her shy smile and smiled back. He rubbed his chin.

"You actually remind me of Gaby," he said to her. "She was a superb writer and she connected with the animals. She also stood up for herself. I bet you just wanted a chance to prove you could do it, didn't you?"

The knot that was crammed in her throat loosened. Tears formed in her eyes. It felt good that someone understood, especially because it was Dr. Villalobos who believed in her. She let out a few sniffles and Spike jumped onto her lap. He licked her chin a few times and then settled himself on her lap as if he was saying that he was on Team Lety.

"Wow," Dr. Villalobos said. "Spike doesn't want you to be sad. I don't either. I think I understand everything now."

Lety wiped a tear streaming down her cheek and gave Spike a kiss on one of his ears. Dr. Villalobos gazed down at the floor for a long time. Lety watched him, wondering if he was trying to decide their punishment.

"Please, don't kick us out like you did with Gaby," Lety blurted. "I really love writing for the animals."

"I don't want to be kicked out either. My grandma paid a lot for this camp," Hunter said.

"Wait? What? Who told you that?" Dr. V. asked.

"One of the other campers," Hunter explained. Dr. Villalobos shook his head slowly, but Hunter continued. "That's why she's not volunteering this summer."

"I wouldn't kick anyone out unless they were maliciously hurting our animals," Dr. Villalobos said. "Gaby loved the animals. She was deeply connected to all of them. They weren't a game or a contest to her."

Lety felt a pang of guilt. She wanted the chance to tell Dr. V. that Spike was not a game or contest for her.

"Gaby made a wrong decision. It was a misunderstanding. She thought she was saving a cat's life. She's not here this summer because she went to visit her mom. I would never kick her out and I'm not going to kick you guys out either."

Hunter exhaled hard, as if he'd been holding his breath the entire time. Lety felt relieved as the lump in her throat disappeared.

"I have to know you can work together and that you are here to help the animals. Our animals are not a contest. They need real families and homes."

"I'm sorry, Dr. Villalobos," Lety said. "I want to help the animals find homes. I really do." Telling the truth was like a cool breeze on her warm face. She hoped Dr. Villalobos believed her. Spike gazed up at her with his brown eyes and barked as if saying he believed her with his whole heart.

Dr. Villalobos chuckled.

"Spike and I believe you," Dr. Villalobos said. "But to ensure that you both have learned a lesson, you two will help out in the pantry. Mario and Kennedy will join you after I've had a chance to talk to them later today."

"But it was just me," Hunter rushed to say. "It really was me. No one else."

"I know they were just as much part of the contest as you two. They'll join you. We have the Wags and Whiskers Community Fest coming up and we're giving away five hundred bags of pet food. For the rest of your time here, you can help with that. AND I still need more profiles. Please get started on profiles for Riley and Ailis. Deal?"

Lety and Hunter nodded.

"Drop the fancy words. Focus on writing wonderful profiles. Our furry friends deserve that. You guys can go straight to the food pantry for now. They're expecting you."

Lety grabbed Spike into her arms and kissed him one more time. She placed him down on the ground. She turned to leave with Hunter, relieved that they weren't being kicked out.

"Lety," Dr. Villalobos called out to her. "Your profile for Lorca is your best yet."

"Thank you," she said, glancing down at Spike. She hoped Dr. Villalobos saw that regardless of the contest, she was definitely fit to be Spike's forever family.

"You found a way to use 'supersonic'?" Hunter asked as they walked out of the clinic.

Lety nodded.

"I was wrong about you," he said, and shook his head. "Really wrong." Lety didn't know how to respond, so she remained quiet as they walked side by side to the pet food pantry.

CHAPTER 19

Long Gone

While all of the other kids watched a demonstration about K-9 dogs outside, Lety and Hunter stood over a large barrel full of dry dog food. They wore aprons and oversized yellow rubber gloves. Lety and Hunter went to work fast, barely saying anything to each other. Soon, the only sound in the pantry was Lety and Hunter's constant scooping and filling of plastic bags.

Lety wasn't sure where things stood with Hunter anymore. She still couldn't believe he'd apologized to her, but now he didn't even look at her. She wondered if he felt guilty for — as he said — being off the mark about her. She wanted to break the silence between them but wasn't sure how. The last time he'd spoken more than ten words to her was when he was talking about his dog, Gunner. Yet she knew Gunner, for some reason, was a sad subject for him. She wasn't sure she should bring it back up. She thought back to the day that she saw him outside waiting for his ride from the shelter.

"You live with your grandma?" Lety asked.

"I do now," Hunter said.

"You didn't before?"

Hunter shrugged and was silent for a few seconds.

"It's because my parents got divorced," Hunter said. "My mom, me, and my little brothers moved in with my grandma because my dad refused to leave our house."

Lety's mouth gaped open. "Sorry, that sounds bad," she said.

"It is bad and it keeps getting worse," Hunter said with a scowl.

"What do you mean?"

"It's my dad doing what he always does," Hunter said with another shrug. "He kept my Gunner because he was mad at my mom. Then a couple of weeks ago, he gave Gunner to my uncle Steve in Wichita. He didn't tell me or anything. He said he was tired of my mom getting after him about returning the dog to us. He said it would be easier for everyone if he just gave the dog away to someone else because we didn't have any money, but he's the stupid reason we don't have money anymore. And I didn't . . ." Hunter's voice trailed off and another familiar shrug followed.

Lety dipped her scoop hard into the dry dog food.

"Didn't what?"

"I didn't even get to give her a kiss good-bye."

"That's awful. Can you get her back?"

"I don't know."

"What? She's your dog. You have to get her back."

"I know, but what happened was that my grandma called my uncle and asked him to return Gunner to us. He said he took the dog to a shelter. He said Gunner was tearing things up in his house." Hunter shook his head, like he was shaking off the memory of that conversation. "The thing is, Gunner never tore things up at our house. She's a good dog. I think it's because she didn't want to be with him. She wanted to be with us."

"She missed you," Lety added. "That's why she acted up."

Hunter nodded in agreement. "I think that's what it was. Anyway, my uncle says he doesn't remember the name of the shelter so my grandma is calling as many shelters as she can during her breaks at work. My mom is calling, too, but there are a lot of shelters in Wichita."

Lety searched for the right words to say to Hunter. His story made her stomach twist. It was the worst story she'd ever heard. It felt almost as bad as the man yelling at them at the store.

"That is why you were staring at Sawyer. You miss your dog."

"Every morning . . ." Hunter said, his face turning crimson. "I think of her every morning and night because she used to sleep in my bed with me. Before I went to bed, I'd read a story to her and my little brothers. We would tell her, 'Choose a book, Gunner.' And she'd take a book from the shelf with her mouth and bring it to us. Drove my mom nuts, but she was super smart."

Lety wondered if that's why Hunter was such a good writer and reader. He was reading books every night to his dog and baby brothers.

"When I wake up and think of her, I wonder if she wakes up thinking of me. Do you think dogs do that? Wake up and think of us?"

"Yes, I do," Lety answered as tears started rimming her eyes just thinking of Gunner far away — maybe in a cage at some shelter in Wichita — wondering when Hunter was going to show up and take her home. "I bet Gunner thinks about you and smiles in her own doggy way. You know how dogs stretch their mouths back and kind of pant like they're laughing?"

"Oh yeah, she would do that all the time," Hunter said.

"I bet that is what she is doing right now at that shelter. She knows you're looking for her and smiles."

Hunter was silent.

"I hope so," he said finally. "Anyway, that's why I'm here. My grandma enrolled me to get my mind off of my dad and Gunner. And I know this will sound bad, but the contest with you sort of helped."

Lety nodded. "I understand."

"I knew it was wrong. I really did. My mom and grandma say I've been a pint-sized jerk lately."

Lety let out a laugh, surprised that Hunter would admit being called a jerk.

"And I was thinking . . ." Hunter continued. "You should write all of the profiles from now on. Yours are way better than mine."

Lety's mouth dropped open in shock. Hunter chuckled.

"I mean it," he said.

"I've been thinking yours are better. I almost quit after reading your profile on Kenzie."

"No way." Hunter shook his head. "That Chicharito profile was really good. Especially the way you tied it in with soccer. Mario liked it, too. He just won't tell you."

"Thanks," Lety said, wishing so much that Kennedy and Brisa were there to hear everything. "I liked your profile about Kenzie and Brooks. Those are two of my favorites."

"So what should we do, then?"

"Can't we just keep sharing them? I'll take Ailis, the poodle, and you can take Riley."

"Works for me. I can't wait to see what you come up with next."

"I see barrels and barrels of pet food. That's what is coming up next."

Hunter laughed.

"I do have an idea for another project here at the shelter. Do you want to hear it?"

"For sure," Hunter said. Lety dug deep into the bucket of dog food. She'd never imagined that a bucket full of beef-flavored dog food would bring Hunter Farmer and her together on the same side. She spent the rest of the morning telling him what happened to her and Brisa at the store, and her idea to get Brisa back to the shelter and help all the furry friends find their forever homes. By the time she was done explaining, Hunter said he'd help. That is, if she wanted his help.

She did.

CHAPTER 20

Lety's Big Idea

The next day, Hunter and Lety faced another full barrel of dog food when Kennedy and Mario trudged into the pantry wearing aprons and oversized yellow rubber gloves.

"My hair is going to smell!" Kennedy whined. "This is gross."

"You can wear this shower cap," Hunter said, pulling a transparent hair cap out from his apron pocket. Lety giggled, knowing that Kennedy would be annoyed at his silly offer.

"Yeah, right," Kennedy growled, pulling her long, wavy hair back into a ponytail. After a few seconds of watching Lety show them how to scoop pet food into bags and then tie the bags, Kennedy went at it like there was gold at the bottom of the barrel.

"This ain't a contest, Kennedy," Hunter said.

"What?" she asked. "Speaking of contest . . . Mario and I talked with Dr. Villalobos, and we decided that you deserved an apology, Lety."

Lety glanced over at Kennedy and Mario, confused.

"For what?" She filled a bag with pet food and tied it.

"I was all crazed poodle about this contest because I was still mad at Mario. I shouldn't have encouraged it. You know how I am. I just wanted Mario and Hunter to shut up already."

"Nice language," Mario quipped.

Lety smiled at her best friend. "It's okay. I know how you are."

"Kennedy is holding a grudge. She's still mad about the soccer game last year when she touched the ball with her hand to get a goal and I called her on it."

"Whatever, Mario," Kennedy said. "We still beat your team two to one."

"Should have been one to one. Anyway, the contest was my idea. So I want to say I'm sorry, too. I just wanted to help out my boy Hunter because he wanted to be shelter scribe and he didn't want your help. Sorry, Lety. I deserve a yellow card."

"More like a red card," Kennedy added.

Lety stared down at the pet food. She wasn't sure what to make of all these apologies. In English, there were so many ways to apologize. If Lety needed to get through a crowd in the school hallway, she'd say, "Excuse me." If Lety couldn't understand someone and needed them to speak slower, Lety used "Pardon me?" and if, by chance, she hurt someone's feelings, she'd say, "Sorry." The best part of saying *sorry* was it was almost always followed by another word she liked: *forgive*. And forgiveness meant moving on with her friends Kennedy, Mario, and Hunter. She only wished that Brisa were with her to see and hear all of it.

"I forgive you," she said.

"But that's not everything," Hunter added.

"You're going to tell them?" Mario said. He shook his head. "This is going to get ugly." He moved away from Kennedy and closer to Hunter.

"What?" Lety asked. "What else?"

"We were at Mario's house playing video games and we came up with all these stupid words for you. Even though it wasn't part of the deal we made. We changed the —"

"I knew it!" Kennedy said, holding her metal scoop up in a threatening way. "You guys changed the rules!"

"Guilty as charged," Mario admitted. "That's a penalty for sure."

"Augh!" Kennedy shook her head and angrily dipped her scooper into the barrel.

"I knew you changed the rules," Lety said. "I went along with it because I wanted to win fair and square. No extra help."

"I'm sorry," Hunter said. "I got caught up in the contest. My mom says if I don't sweeten up, Gunner won't want to come home to me —" Hunter's voice broke, stopping Kennedy and Mario mid-scoop.

"Dude, you all right?" Mario asked.

Hunter shrugged.

Lety thought back to every rude comment Hunter had made to her, and in her head she made a list. One by one she deleted each insult and replaced it with each new kind gestured he'd made: the smile he gave her after the Rescue Team presentation, his apology in front of Dr. Villalobos, standing up for her with Mario about the contest, and now helping her with her new idea.

"I forgive you, Hunter," she said finally. "Again."

A smiled crossed Hunter's face. "I'm going to help get Brisa back to the shelter. If I don't want people to be a jerk to you and Brisa, I should start with myself."

"Whoa, Hunter," Kennedy said. "That's, like . . . mature."

"You said your dog was taken to a shelter in Wichita, right?" Lety asked. Hunter nodded. "Have you thought about asking Dr. Villalobos for help? I bet he knows the other animal shelters there. Maybe he can make a call and help bring Gunner home?"

Hunter's brown eyes shined.

"Why didn't I think of that?" he asked. "I'd give you a hug, Lety, but I smell like lamb chunks."

"Who cares, dude!" Mario laughed. "She smells like lamb chunks, too."

"We all do now," Kennedy added.

Hunter slipped off his yellow rubber gloves and leaned in for a hug, extending his arms wide open around Lety. Mario and Kennedy joined them and made it a sloppy group hug. Lety couldn't remember ever being so happy that she'd given someone a second chance.

CHAPTER 21

Reading Fur Friends

After an hour of shoveling dry dog food into bags, Lety and Hunter went to see Dr. Villalobos. They found him in the clinic. At his feet, Spike chewed on a squeaky toy.

"Spike!" Lety squealed. Spike padded over to Lety and Hunter. Lety bent down to give him a good pet and a couple of kisses on his muzzle. "My favorite dog!" She dug into her pocket and pulled out a doggy treat. "Is it okay?" she asked Dr. Villalobos. He nodded.

"Is Spike ready to be adopted yet?" Hunter asked, passing a sly glance over to Lety.

"Almost," Dr. Villalobos answered.

Lety smiled, thinking of her own family and wondering if Dr. Villalobos had forgiven her enough to let her adopt Spike.

"So what can I do for you guys? Everything good in the pantry?"

"Hunter and I finished another fifty bags this morning," Lety said. "Kennedy and Mario are still scooping away. We wanted to talk to you about a couple of things."

"What's up?"

Hunter cleared his throat and told his story about Gunner. He even pulled out his phone and showed Dr. Villalobos a couple of photos. By time he was done, Dr. Villalobos was on the phone with Daisy, asking her to call the Humane Society. Hunter emailed a photo of Gunner to Daisy.

"We'll do our best to find Gunner," Dr. Villalobos said. "I'm so sorry that happened to you."

"Thank you," Hunter said. "Now it's Lety's turn. She has a really good idea."

"Talk to me, Lety."

"Do you remember my friend Brisa? She doesn't come anymore to the shelter?"

"Yeah, I heard it was something to do with her mom being pregnant. Is that right?"

"No, it wasn't that at all," Lety continued. "Well, her mom is pregnant, but the truth is Brisa, me, her mom, and my baby brother went to the store last week and something bad happened. Brisa was translating for her mom at the pharmacy. The pharmacist was speaking Spanish, too, and this man in line behind them became upset. He started yelling at them that this was America and to speak English."

"What? That's horrible." Dr. Villalobos shook his head in disgust.

"I know," Lety said. "It was awful. Afterward, Brisa said she had to focus on her English, so she went back to summer school, but she misses the cats like crazy. And I miss her, too."

"I wish someone would have told me," Dr. V. said. "Maybe I could have talked to her and convinced her stay with us at the camp. I would have liked to have helped."

"You can still help, Dr. V.," Lety said, grateful that Dr. Villalobos had made the offer.

She took a deep breath and remembered her lines from when she practiced in front of the mirror at home. "This whole experience gave me an idea for a program that I'd like to start here, with your permission. It could help lots of kids, like me, who are learning English, and provide company to the shelter pets who spend so many hours alone in their cages."

Spike dropped his squeaky toy at her feet and barked twice. Lety laughed.

"Spike likes it already," said Dr. Villalobos.

"What if we could devote a morning or afternoon every week for a program called Reading FUR Friends? For a couple of hours a day, kids like Brisa and my younger brother could come in and read to the dogs and cats."

"I used to read to my Gunner all the time," Hunter added. "She loved it."

"I'm prepared to do a demonstration for you with the cat burritos if you'd like," Lety said. "I brought a book."

"That's not necessary." Dr. Villalobos smiled. He rubbed his chin. "I've heard of a similar program at a shelter in Chicago. It's been successful. I like it. Let's do it."

"Really?" Lety asked.

"Of course! What do we need to do to make it happen?"

Lety's head buzzed with excitement and next steps.

"We need to talk to Mrs. Camacho. She's my teacher. Maybe she can make it part of their summer program? I think she'll agree because she has two rescue cats."

"Woman after my own heart," Dr. V. said. "Leave me Mrs. Camacho's email and I'll contact her. Seriously, Lety. It's a great idea."

Lety and Hunter left Dr. V.'s office, feeling on top of the world. They didn't even notice that Spike followed them out. Lety and Hunter met up with Kennedy and Mario in the multipurpose room. Each of them agreed to donate books from their homes. If Lety had a tail, it would have definitely been wagging. Luckily for her, Spike was close by and doing enough wagging for the both of them.

CHAPTER 22

A Thousand Chances

On Saturday afternoon, the girls gathered at Kennedy's pool. Lety was anxious to see Brisa. She'd talked to her a few times over the phone, but she hadn't seen her friend the entire week and she missed her. Plus, she couldn't wait to tell her the plan for the Reading FUR Friends project.

"Isn't that a fun name?" Kennedy said, slathering her freckled shoulders with sunblock. "Genius, really."

Brisa spread her beach towel over the lounge chair and remained quiet. She gazed out over the blue pool in front of them. Her silence was not the reaction Lety had expected. Lety wanted Brisa to like the idea.

"Brisa?" Lety said.

"And Dr. V. was okay with it?" Brisa asked.

"He thinks it rocks," Lety answered. "Daisy, too. They think if it goes well, they can make it a permanent program throughout the year. It's good for the animals and it's good for everyone to practice reading. Not just girls like us learning English."

"Mrs. Camacho?"

"Loves it!" Lety said, starting to feel like she had to defend her idea to Brisa. "I emailed her and she's already making plans to bring you guys on Tuesday."

"Tuesday?" Brisa asked.

"¿Qué tienes, Brisa?" Lety asked. "Why aren't you hooting for joy or dancing around with excitement like usual?"

"Yeah. More hooting. Less pouty questions," Kennedy added. "You should be totally happy. You get to see the cats again."

Brisa chewed on her lip a bit and then sat up in the chair to face Lety and Kennedy.

"I'm worried. Is Hunter going to be around reading, too,

with his superior reading skills? I don't want to look like a baby reading a baby book in front of him."

"You can bring any book you want," Lety said. "We'll also have books at the shelter for you to choose from."

"Plus, things have changed with Hunter and Lety," Kennedy said, removing her sunglasses. "They're sweethearts now."

Lety's mouth gaped open, and she shook her head. She scrambled to find something to throw at Kennedy but found nothing, so she dipped the tips of her feet in the pool and splashed Kennedy. Kennedy shrieked and laughed.

"*¡Ay, dios mío!*" Brisa gasped. "Hunter?"

"We are friends. He apologized for being rude. And he said he thought my animal profiles were better than his."

"He admitted that?" Kennedy asked.

"Wow! What else did I miss?" Brisa said.

"You don't have to miss anything anymore, Brisa. On Tuesday, you can be back with us and practice English while helping all the furry friends."

Brisa smiled wide. "As my mom would say, 'I have *tinkaso* about this new idea of yours.'"

"*Tinkaso?* Is that Spanish?" Kennedy asked.

"Not Spanish. It's Quechua," Brisa answered. "My grandma speaks it, and she and my mom use *tinkaso* whenever they have a good gut feeling about something."

"So then you like my idea?" Lety pressed, relieved that Brisa was finally on board with the new program.

"Yes, I like it and I can't wait to return to the shelter to see all the *gatitos* again."

"Yay! I have *tinkaso* about your program, too," Kennedy practiced the new word. And "I have *tinkaso* that Ailis the poodle will be adopted soon. Your profile is on point. Big time."

"Thanks," Lety said.

"Read it to me, Kennedy," Brisa said. "I love that sweet poodle with her little *chuño* nose."

Kennedy grabbed her iPhone and read the profile from the website.

"Best dog profile ever!" Brisa gushed.

"And what about Spike?" Kennedy asked.

Brisa and Kennedy both looked at Lety. They knew she had loved Spike since that first day at the shelter.

"Don't you want to adopt him for you and Eddie?" Kennedy asked. "You guys would be the perfect family. I told Dr. V."

"You did? What did he say?" Lety asked.

"He smiled real big and said he'd be happy if someone like you were Spike's family. I think he's just waiting for you to say something."

"Do it!" Brisa squealed so loud that it sent a couple of birds on the roof of the pool house darting off into the sky.

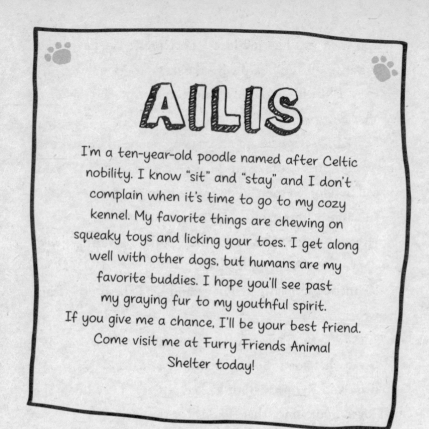

AILIS

I'm a ten-year-old poodle named after Celtic nobility. I know "sit" and "stay" and I don't complain when it's time to go to my cozy kennel. My favorite things are chewing on squeaky toys and licking your toes. I get along well with other dogs, but humans are my favorite buddies. I hope you'll see past my graying fur to my youthful spirit. If you give me a chance, I'll be your best friend. Come visit me at Furry Friends Animal Shelter today!

"Okay, we'll see," Lety said. She thought about the profile for Spike that the previous shelter scribe, Gaby, had written. The last line asked for someone to take a chance on him. Lety was willing to give him a thousand chances. For her, he was still the smartest dog she'd ever met.

ChAPTeR 23

Books and Buddies

On Tuesday, Hunter's hands were filled with picture books about dinosaurs and sharks. Mario brought his whole collection of Harry Potter paperbacks. Kennedy had a book filled with Irish folktales to share.

"This will be just like how I used to read to Gunner," Hunter said to Lety, showing her the books he'd brought. "I'm going to start by reading to Finn. I think he'd like this story about a shark who wants to make friends, but all the other fish are scared of him."

"That sounds good," Lety said. "Does he end up making friends?"

Hunter looked into Lety's brown eyes. "It's a total happy ending."

And the way he said it made Lety feel like maybe Hunter and she were a happy ending, too. Two weeks ago, she would never have thought they could be friends, but here they were talking books and working on animal profiles together.

Then right on time, the front door of the shelter swung open and Brisa raced in. Behind her, Mrs. Camacho entered, leading a group of familiar faces that Lety knew. Mrs. Camacho's silver-gray hair was pulled back into a chignon, and she wore a T-shirt with a long floral skirt. The T-shirt read: SOY BILINGÜE. WHAT'S YOUR SUPERPOWER? Brisa quickly embraced Lety like she hadn't seen her in a hundred years.

"I can't believe I'm back! I'm so happy!" Brisa exclaimed. "I will read to all the cats."

Eddie walked in, chatting it up with Gazi and Aziza and a couple of younger boys Lety didn't know yet. He clutched paint swatches in his small hands. His eyes gazed over the room and then stopped when he saw Lety. He smiled and waved the swatches at her.

"What colors did you bring?" Lety asked, giving him a kiss on his head.

"I brought all the colors. Sunflower Smile, Dandelion Gold, Creamy Meringue . . ." Eddie said as Lety shuffled through the swatches. "I'm going to read them to the cats. Do you think the cats will like it, Lety?"

"Of course! What cat wouldn't want to hear the latest paint colors?"

Eddie looked down at his swatches. "Good. That's what I thought, too. I also want to read some of your profiles. Can Santiago and me read them, Lety?"

"I'll print some out for you."

Soon, Dr. Villalobos swaggered into the room, smiling over the mix of English learners and summer campers gathered together. He crossed the room to shake hands with Mrs. Camacho and surprised everyone when he started speaking Spanish to her. Brisa's eyes grew wide.

"Dr. Villalobos speaks Spanish, too?" she asked Lety.

"I had no idea," Lety said, and then she giggled after listening for a bit.

"What's he saying?" Kennedy asked.

"They're talking about the animal profiles and Lety's idea," Brisa said, and then she laughed. "His accent is funny, but his Spanish is good. Right, Lety?"

Lety nodded. Dr. Villalobos spotted Lety and waved her over. Lety walked over with Eddie and Brisa. Once there, Mrs. Camacho put an arm around Lety's shoulders.

"I'm so proud of you," she said. "Lety's one of our best students. I'm not surprised that she's writing animal profiles and starting new programs."

Lety looked up at Mrs. Camacho's light brown eyes and smiled back.

"She always has good ideas," Eddie said.

"That's because kids who learn new languages are natural problem solvers, Eduardo," Mrs. Camacho said. "Just like you."

"I know that," Eddie said. Lety patted his head like he was a puppy.

"Welcome, everyone!" Dr. Villalobos faced the entire group. "Welcome to Furry Friends Animal Shelter!"

A sudden tingle went up and down Lety's arms, leaving her with goose bumps. Her idea to bring her friends from school and the animals at the shelter together was really happening! Brisa must have sensed her excitement because she gave Lety's hand a squeeze.

Soon, the campers and the ELL students were split up into four groups. One group, led by Dr. Villalobos and another adult volunteer, went to the Bow Wow Zone to read to the big dogs like Finn and Riley. Hunter waved to Lety as he left with this group. Another group, led by Alma, went to the small-dog room. Finally, the last two groups followed Daisy into the Feline Friends room, clutching books in their hands.

Students laid out carpet remnants in front of the cages and opened their books and slowly began reading. Brisa read to Kiwi, who was the last remaining cat of her entire litter. Kennedy read Irish folktales to a large cat who was eight years old and showed no signs of finding her forever family. Eddie read paint swatch after paint swatch to a litter of white kittens who reached out their little paws to him and mewed impatiently. Lety gazed over the group reading to the cats, feeling proud when she felt someone's stare. Spike was on the other side of the glass door, looking in at her. Lety got up and went outside to where he sat perfectly straight. She shook her head at the idea that anyone would think he was too wild. He wasn't too wild. He was perfect!

"You want to hear a story, Spike?" she asked. As if Spike understood and really wanted a story, he wagged his tail and twitched his ears. Lety swooped him up into her arms and pressed her face against his fur.

"I'm going to read to you a story about this beautiful princess and warrior in ancient Mexico. Would you like that?"

Spike yelped excitedly. Lety knew this was dog language for: "Yes, read to me." She grabbed a picture book from the donation box, sat down on a chair in the reception area, and began to read.

CHAPTER 24

Purrfect Success!

"We're going to be on the news!" Kennedy shrieked.

Lety took a deep breath as the news van parked outside the shelter.

"Now, don't worry, Lety," Dr. Villalobos said. "They want to hear all about the program. You'll be fine as long as you speak from your heart."

At first, Lety had tried to get out of the interview, but Dr. Villalobos wouldn't have it. He said she deserved the credit, but Lety was nervous about speaking on TV. She smoothed down her teal-blue camp shirt.

"It's just sometimes when I get nervous, my accent comes out," Lety said to Kennedy and Hunter.

"So what?" Hunter said. "I like the way you talk."

Brisa rushed out of the cat room toward them with a picture book in her hand. "You'll never believe this, but Solo and Sinclair love books about fishes. So we need more books about sharks, swordfish, manatees, starfish. All the wonders of the ocean!"

"Maybe we can collect books at the Wags and Whiskers event," Hunter offered.

"Good idea," Lety said. "We can ask the reporter today to mention it."

The reporter from the local station was a petite brunette with rosy pink lips and cheeks. The campers rushed up to her for an autograph as soon as she arrived until Dr. Villalobos ushered them away. She and the cameraman set themselves up inside the cat room to take footage of the Reading FUR Friends program in action.

At one point, Lorca took an interest in the camera and swiped at it with his paw, which made everyone laugh.

After they took their footage of the campers reading to various animals, the reporter talked to Lety and Hunter.

"How did you come up with this idea to read to the animals?" the reporter asked Lety.

"I had a friend who wanted to volunteer at the shelter, but she also wanted to practice her English at summer school. I thought this program, Reading FUR Friends, would be a way to do both: improve reading while helping the animals."

"And you?" The reporter turned the microphone to Hunter. "What are you reading to the dogs today?"

"I have a book here called *La Gallinita Roja*. Did I say that right, Lety?"

"Really good." She smiled. It was a book she had known as a child, but she never expected Hunter to have a copy.

"Why Spanish?" the reporter asked.

"My friends, like Lety, want to practice English, but I think it's important that we all try to learn new languages."

"And do the dogs like your Spanish book?"

"That's the cool thing. Dogs and cats don't care what language you speak or read. They just want to hear your voice and be close to you. That's all that matters."

"There you have it! This young lady, Lety Muñoz, has really started something wonderful at Furry Friends Animal Shelter, and kids like Hunter Farmer are making it a purrfect success! Don't forget the Wags and Whiskers Community Fest event this weekend. Stop by to donate a book, read to a furry friend, and maybe adopt a new member of your family. I'm Amanda Velasco with Channel Five News."

"Good job, you two," she said. "You know, my daughter and I adopted a kitten from here. His name is Secret. Starting tomorrow, I'm going to read to him. You've truly inspired me." As she rushed off to shake hands with Dr. Villalobos and Daisy, Lety grabbed Hunter's book.

"Where did you get this?" she asked.

"My grandma got it for me. She knows I want to learn Spanish."

"Really?"

"Sure; this way I can talk to you in Spanish and the other kids at school who speak Spanish. I want to try at least. You think it'll work?"

Lety opened the book. Even in Mexico, she had never owned a book in Spanish. Books were too expensive for her family to buy. She gazed over the Spanish words that now seemed so far away, like her home in Tlaquepaque. Hunter watched her.

"I've never owned a book in Spanish."

"What? That's nuts! You want to borrow it?" Hunter asked. "Or if you want, we can read it together?"

Lety smiled at him, trying not to blush. The more time she spent with Hunter, the more he surprised her with his kindness.

"Okay," she said, just as Dr. Villalobos approached them.

"Fantastic job on the interview. Can I speak to you both in the cat room?"

Inside the cat room, Daisy held Lorca.

"We found Gunner," Dr. Villalobos announced, but he said it in such a serious manner that Lety sucked in her breath. The tone of his voice didn't sound like it was total good news.

"Is she okay?" Hunter asked.

"Yes, she's perfectly fine," Daisy said in the same serious tone that Dr. Villalobos used. "Our friend in Wichita shared your picture with all of the animal shelters. As soon as he did, one of the shelters recognized Gunner," said Daisy. "Unfortunately, they reported that a family with two boys adopted her a week ago."

"What?" Hunter said. His face flushed ruby-red so fast that Lety wanted to reach out and grab his hand, but then he put his hands up over his face in disbelief. "Adopted?"

"We're so sorry," Daisy said.

"Look, Hunter, I've already spoken to the director at the shelter. I explained everything. And he's willing to speak to the family on your behalf. We both believe that if the family knew the situation with Gunner, they'd give her back to you. I think it's worth a try."

This made Lety feel better. Surely, if the family knew the truth about how Gunner had been taken from Hunter, they'd understand.

Hunter stood quiet behind his hands.

"It's all my dad's fault," he said. He uncovered his face. "Now she's gone forever."

"That's not true," Dr. Villalobos said. "When your grandma comes to pick you up, why don't you bring her and the boys inside." Dr. Villalobos put his hands on Hunter's shoulders. "Listen, don't lose hope. We can discuss next steps. Okay?"

Hunter shrugged. "Okay." He walked out of the cat room into the reception area and slumped down on a bench. Lety joined him.

"I'm sorry, Hunter," she said. "What are you going to do?"

"I don't know," Hunter said. "On one hand, she's my dog. I should get her back, but then I don't want to separate other kids from their new dog. I don't want to be like my dad."

Lety stared down at her hands, unsure of what to say. She didn't know his dad, but what she knew of him sounded nothing like Hunter.

"You deserve to have her back. She's your dog."

"What if they love her as much as I do? Maybe Gunner is happy with them. It's been almost three weeks, going on four away from us. That's not long to humans, but for dogs that's a big chunk of their lives." Hunter gazed out the window just as his grandma's tan car pulled up. "My grandma is here. I have to tell her to come in. See you tomorrow?"

Lety shook her head. "Don't give up, Hunter."

"Thanks. Bye, Lety."

Hunter rushed out the door toward his grandma's car. He directed her to park. Lety's mom showed up, too. Lety took her seat in the back with Eddie. As her mom drove away, Hunter waved to her. She opened her notebook and began to write.

CHAPTER 25

The Man in the Red Hat

The Bow Wow Zone buzzed with the sounds of children reading. Brisa and her classmates were back.

"I have an idea, Lety," Brisa said, closing a picture book about dinosaurs. "You should start adding book recommendations to the animal profiles. Finn and Riley like books about sharks."

"Good idea. I noticed that Solo likes to be read the

newspaper — especially the sports section. She purrs and purrs when I read about soccer," Lety said, pulling her profile for Solo out of her pocket. "Let's add it and see what Dr. V. thinks."

Brisa passed her a pen from her pocket. Lety added a couple of lines.

"What do you think?" She read the profile to Brisa.

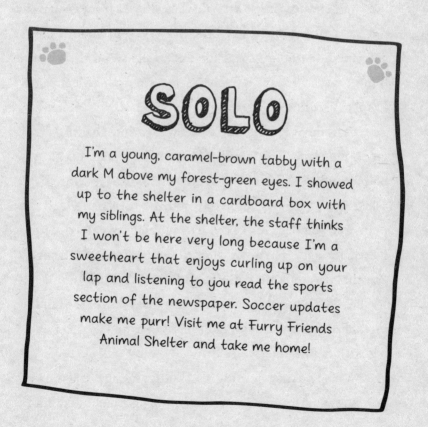

SOLO

I'm a young, caramel-brown tabby with a dark M above my forest-green eyes. I showed up to the shelter in a cardboard box with my siblings. At the shelter, the staff thinks I won't be here very long because I'm a sweetheart that enjoys curling up on your lap and listening to you read the sports section of the newspaper. Soccer updates make me purr! Visit me at Furry Friends Animal Shelter and take me home!

Suddenly, Finn jumped from his bed and started barking at a man wearing a red baseball cap. Brisa and Lety looked up toward the man and realized they had seen him before.

"*¡No puede ser!*" Brisa gasped. She leaned in and whispered to Lety. "It's the angry man from the store."

At first, Lety wasn't sure. His back was to her, but when he turned to face one of the little girls, she knew those blue eyes and strands of brown hair that strayed from under his red baseball hat. He walked by with two girls about Eddie's age and didn't notice Brisa and Lety. Lety stood there trembling and grabbed Brisa's hand for strength. Meanwhile, Finn kept barking.

"Easy, boy," Hunter said. "Who's wearing a hat? Oh, that guy." He glanced at Lety and did a double take. Lety's eyes blazed into the back of the man's head. "What's wrong?" he asked her. When she didn't answer, he turned back to the man and tapped his shoulder. Hunter explained Finn's hatred for hats. The man laughed, which made Lety angry. But the man took his hat off and Finn settled down.

Lety felt a tug at her sleeve. She looked down. One of the man's little girls was pulling on her sleeve and looking up at her with ocean-blue eyes.

"Why are they reading to the dogs?" she asked Lety, pointing at Gazi and Aziza sitting in front of Riley's and Finn's cage with books in their hands. The man turned around and faced Lety. He showed no signs that he recognized her.

"We started a new program here called Reading FUR Friends," Lety explained.

"I like that name," said one of the girls, shoving her purple-rimmed glasses farther up on her freckled face.

"It helps kids who are learning English. And it helps the dogs to not feel so alone in their cages."

"I want to do that!" squealed one of the girls.

"Me, too!" shouted the other girl.

"Do you want to read to Finn?" Brisa added, looking directly at the man. Suddenly, his face twitched with recognition. He made a rapid head turn from Brisa to Lety. There was no denying that he remembered them now. Lety met his gaze. At that moment, everything she and Brisa had talked about telling the man pushed up against her heart and made its way to her mouth, but the words came to a halt at her lips when the little girl with the glasses spoke.

"I want to read to the dogs, Dad. Can I?"

"No, we're going." He grabbed both girls' hands and rushed them out of the room. Hunter shook his head at the suddenness of the man's departure.

"What the heck? Did he get a call that his house was on fire or something?"

Lety and Brisa stood there, shocked.

"He has daughters," Brisa said. "Sweet *muñecas*."

"How is it possible that someone like that could have sweet girls?" Lety asked.

"What's going on?" Hunter asked. "Did you know that guy?"

Brisa and Lety nodded simultaneously.

"Unfortunately," Brisa said.

"Remember that guy I told you about?" Lety said. "The one who yelled at us to speak English because we were in America?"

"No way," Hunter said. He looked toward the door where the man and his daughters had exited. "He can't leave. He needs to apologize right now." Hunter dashed out after the man.

"Hunter! What are you doing?" Lety yelled after him, but he was gone.

CHAPTER 26

We Go High

The man in the red baseball hat was long gone. Lety sat in the reception area, between Brisa and Hunter. Dr. Villalobos hovered over them, worried about how quiet Lety had become. Spike sat on her lap and licked her folded hands.

"Are you okay, Lety?" Dr. Villalobos asked her for the third time that morning after Hunter had told everyone what transpired in the Bow Wow Zone.

"You're not mad that I couldn't catch him, are you?" Hunter asked.

Lety shook her head and then giggled, imagining Hunter demanding an apology from the man outside in the parking lot.

"I cannot believe you chased him," Brisa said.

"All the way out the parking lot," Dr. Villalobos added. "That guy was in his car and I spotted Hunter out there, waving his arms trying to get him to stop."

Brisa laughed. *"Estás loco,* Hunter."

"I know what that means, and I guess it does seem a little crazy. I just wanted to say something to him. I don't know why. Does it make me crazy?"

"It makes you a good friend," Lety said. If there was ever anything bad between them, she knew now it was 100 percent gone. It felt good.

"I'm very proud of you girls," Dr. Villalobos said. "You could have really gone off on that guy. I know you wanted to, but instead you took the higher road."

"When they go low, we go high," Brisa said. "It's my favorite English expression."

Lety stared down at Spike and gave him a few gentle strokes.

"You're awfully quiet, Lety," Dr. Villalobos said. "What are you thinking about?"

Lety wasn't sure she should say, but Brisa gave her a gentle nudge.

"I thought I'd never want to see that man again. But I'm glad that we did."

"Why?" Hunter asked.

"After all of his yelling and bullying at the store, I'm glad that he knows now that none of that stopped us. We didn't run and hide. We didn't lower our eyes to him. His words didn't stop us from living and doing what we love. Now he knows."

"It almost stopped me," Brisa said. "If it wasn't for the reading program, I wouldn't have come back to the shelter."

"But you're back now," said Dr. Villalobos. "That's what matters."

Brisa hugged Lety and Spike joined in, licking them both on their happy faces until an older couple walked in. One of the men held a paper in his hand. Spike greeted them with a friendly bark.

"Welcome. Can I help you?" Dr. Villalobos asked.

"We would like to adopt this precious cat, Lorca," the man said, dipping down to pet Spike, then handing the printout to Dr. V. "We loved his online profile and we've been looking for a cat to join our family."

"Lorca is a great cat," Brisa said.

Dr. Villalobos quickly escorted them toward the Feline Friends room. As he opened the door, he flashed thumbs-up to Lety.

Lety's heart pounded with joy. Lorca was finally going to have a family.

"You did it," Hunter said. "I told you your profiles were awesome. Maybe you can help me with Riley's?" Hunter pulled out a piece of notebook paper and pen from his back jeans pocket.

"Don't forget to add that he likes books about sharks," Brisa said.

Lety read through the profile. It was perfect as it was. She rearranged a few sentences to slip in Brisa's book recommendation, but that's all. She passed it back to Hunter. He read through it.

RILEY

It was a wintry day when the rescue team found me. I was brought into the shelter and needed surgery. Sadly, my back left leg was so damaged, it had to be amputated. Now I'm a healthy and playful seven-month-old husky with only three legs. Still, it doesn't slow me down! When I'm not playing fetch, I enjoy a good book about sharks because sharks never stop moving. And neither do I! Want to play? Visit me at Furry Friends Animal Shelter today!

"Much better," he said.

Later that morning, Lety and Hunter kissed Lorca good-bye and headed to the food pantry to finish food bags for the Wags and Whiskers Community Fest. Spike followed them. In between scoops, Hunter and Lety would toss a beef kibble, sending Spike leaping into the air to catch it in his mouth.

"I really like what you said about standing up to that man and how it made you feel," Hunter said. He stopped scooping and watched Spike for a long time. Lety wondered if he was thinking about standing up to his father for giving away Gunner. "I want to feel like that, too. This whole Gunner thing is in my head. I'm just so mad about it."

"I don't blame you," Lety said.

"Even if I did get Gunner back, that doesn't change things with my dad, you know?" Hunter said, his voice losing its softness and sounding deeper than she'd ever noticed before.

"I understand," she said.

"He purposely tried to hurt me by giving Gunner away. The truth is he hurt himself, because now I don't trust him. My little brothers don't either. My mom won't take him back. She says she's done."

"What does your grandma say?"

"She says we need time and that someday we will have to forgive him. I don't know about that."

"And Gunner? Is she coming back?"

Hunter shook his head.

"I told Dr. Villalobos," Hunter started to explain, drifting into the soft voice that Lety liked so much. "I can't take Gunner away from that family. I just wouldn't feel right."

Lety looked at Hunter, clutching a scooper full of pet food. He met her gaze.

"Are you sure, Hunter?" she asked. "She's been your dog since you were five." Lety couldn't believe he had made such a hard decision. She wasn't so sure she'd make the same one. Hunter threw another kibble to Spike, who leaped for it. "I wish there were more boys like you," Lety said after a few seconds of silence between them. "More boys like you means less men like the one that bullied us at the store."

"And less guys like my dad," Hunter added. "I'm not going to be like either of them."

Both of them quietly returned to scooping, determined to finish their punishment, which no longer felt like punishment to them.

Chapter 27

Wags and Whiskers

A bright yellow banner touting WAGS AND WHISKERS COMMUNITY FEST wafted high between two oak trees outside the animal shelter. As families streamed onto the shelter grounds, Lety and the other summer campers spread out, helping at various stations. Hunter and Mario were at the pet food pantry table with the coordinator and other volunteers.

They handed out bags of pet food that the kids had assembled over the last few weeks.

Kennedy was with the cat heroes, showing families how to make their own affordable cat toys at home. Lety and Brisa were with Alma, accepting book and blanket donations for the Reading FUR Friends program. They also signed up new readers for the program. In just an hour, ten new readers signed up to help out on Saturday mornings and a pile of new books had been donated.

Mrs. Camacho arrived with her husband, looking to adopt a third cat to join their other two rescue cats. Brisa's parents arrived with Lety's family. Eddie raced up to Lety with their parents trailing behind him. It was a rare treat that her father had Saturday off, and she was anxious to show him all around the shelter. Especially because she wanted him to meet Spike.

"Summer heroes! Time for the group picture!" Dr. Villalobos yelled into a bullhorn.

"Go ahead," Alma said to Lety and Brisa. "Dr. Villalobos loves group pictures. I can watch the table."

Brisa and Lety rushed to where the campers gathered on the grass between the trees. Hunter and Mario joined Brisa, Lety, and Kennedy.

As parents snapped and clicked shot after shot, Kennedy's mom was guiding Lety's and Brisa's moms over to meet some of the other parents. It made Lety feel so good that their moms were finally brave enough to talk to other parents and that the other parents were talking to them, too.

"Attention! May I have your attention, campers?" Dr. Villalobos shouted over the kids talking. "Before we continue with today's activities, I have an important announcement." The kids settled down.

"This has been one of the best camps we've ever had, and it's because we had some really phenomenal participants," Dr. Villalobos said. "One summer hero in particular stood out. She started a new program here that I believe will help lots of animals and kids in our city."

Every camper turned to Lety.

"He's talking about you," Hunter whispered. Lety blushed.

"Lety Muñoz, will you come here and stand with me?"

Everyone started to applaud as Lety walked over to Dr. Villalobos. Hunter shouted a few "woos" and Kennedy and Brisa whistled. Lety was joined by her parents and Eddie.

"What's going on?" Eddie asked. "Are we going to get ice cream?"

"I don't know," Lety said, feeling suddenly nervous at being the center of attention.

"We are so thankful for everything you've done at Furry Friends Animal Shelter, Lety," Dr. Villalobos said. "I've already spoken to your parents about your amazing work and they agreed that you deserve something special."

"We're going to get ice cream!" Eddie shouted.

Dr. Villalobos gestured behind them. Lety turned around. Walking toward her was Alma holding Spike on a leash.

"Do we get a dog?" Eddie yelled excitedly, and jumped up and down. "Whoa! So much cooler than ice cream!"

Lety couldn't believe her eyes. Was Alma adopting Spike or was she bringing Spike to her? Lety still wasn't sure.

"Lety, I can't think of a better person to adopt Spike," Alma said. "He's all yours!" She passed the leash to Lety and gave her a hug.

"Thank you!" Lety gushed. Her parents huddled closer to her and gave her kisses on her cheek. "Are you sure, Dr. Villalobos? We meet all of your strict qualifications?"

"Absolutely." Dr. Villalobos smiled. "You've proven to me over and over that you don't give up. When you weren't sure you could write animal profiles, you wrote your heart out. When your friend Brisa quit the camp, you found a way to bring her back. When Hunter lost his dog, it was your idea to talk to me so that we could contact the shelters. You never give up. Spike needs someone exactly like you."

Lety swooped Spike up into her arms and gave him a smooch on his muzzle.

"I'll never give up on him," she said. She couldn't believe Spike was hers.

"*¡Gracias,* Papá! *¡Gracias,* Mamita!*" Lety cried.

All of the kids gathered around Lety to congratulate her. Hunter gave Spike a kiss on his head.

"Since I don't have a dog anymore, I'd be happy to help you with Spike, you know," Hunter said, giving Spike a good scratch behind his ears. "I can walk him with you and read to him if you want," he continued.

"Thank you, Hunter," Lety said. "Spike and I would like that."

"Group picture!" Dr. Villalobos roared again. The kids gathered around Lety with Spike in her arms and snapped more shots. As cameras clicked away, a family entered through the gate of the shelter's back lawn. A boy held a large white dog on a leash. Lety had seen this dog before. It looked just like Sawyer, but it wasn't. That's when it hit her.

"Hunter!" Lety yelled, but he had already seen them and was bolting toward the dog.

"Gunner! Gunner!"

CHAPTER 28

Shelter Scribe Saves the Day

"Gunner, this is my friend Lety," Hunter said, in between Gunner's excited licks. "Shake hands, girl! Shake hands!" The white fluffy Great Pyrenees held up a paw and Lety shook it. "Wow, she still knows everything I taught her." He directed a gaze back at his grandma. She nodded and wiped her eyes with a tissue.

"You taught her well, baby," she said. Hunter's younger brothers kept their arms flung around Gunner protectively, as if afraid to let her go. Gunner wailed excitedly and licked them all over their faces.

"She's super smart, just like you said," Lety said. More campers began to gather around to see what was going on. "She missed you."

"She's so cute!" Brisa squealed, running her hands through Gunner's fur. Gunner turned over on her back and exposed her belly, which made the kids laugh some more.

"She wants her belly rubbed!" Kennedy cried. "Please tell me you get to keep her."

"We get to keep her forever? Right, Hunter?" asked one of Hunter's brothers.

"I think so," Hunter said, looking off toward where Dr. Villalobos was talking to the family that had brought Gunner. The older boy pulled out a folded piece of paper from his back jeans pocket and showed it to Dr. Villalobos. Dr. V. excitedly gestured toward Lety. Soon the family and Dr. Villalobos were walking toward them.

"Please let it be good news," Brisa said, crossing her fingers.

"Hey, I want to introduce everyone to the Salazar family. They came all the way from Wichita to meet Hunter," said Dr. Villalobos, in a voice that made Lety's heart flip. It was Dr. V.'s excited voice. The same voice he used when he spoke about Spike on the first day. The same tone he used when he said he liked the Reading FUR Friends idea.

A young man stepped forward, holding a folded piece of paper in his hands. "Hi, guys, I'm James. My family and I thought you should know why we came today," he said. "Two weeks ago, we adopted Gunner from an animal shelter. It was what my mom calls love at first sight. But as soon as we got Gunner home, she'd cry every night. We tried leaving the light on for her. We gave her extra treats. My mom and dad even let her sleep in their bed with them, even though she insisted on hogging their pillows."

Everyone laughed.

"Nothing would stop her crying at night. We wondered if she was missing something, like a favorite toy or stuffed animal. Soon, we discovered that Gunner wasn't missing some*thing*. She was missing some*one*. She was missing you, Hunter. You and your family."

Hunter sniffled and Lety quickly patted his back.

"We received a phone call from the shelter director, explaining your story. Then we received Gunner's profile."

"Profile?" Hunter looked confused.

James unfolded the piece of paper he held in his hand and read it out loud.

GUNNER

When I was a four-month-old pup, I was a birthday gift for a little boy named Hunter. The little boy said I looked like a baby white bear. I slept in his bed every night of his life until a few weeks ago when suddenly he was gone and I was alone. Before we were separated, Hunter used to read to me at night. I would choose a book from the shelf and take it to him in my mouth. Hunter would read it in his soft voice that warmed me like a favorite blanket. At night, my doggy dreams were filled with Hunter and me chasing dragons, building rocket blasters, and playing fetch until the cerise sunset sent us back to our beds. I miss my boy Hunter and I know he misses me.

Lety let out a soft smile in recognition. Hunter glanced over at her with moist eyes.

"You?" he asked.

Lety responded with an it-was-the-least-I-could-do shrug.

"Oh, Lety!" Kennedy cried. "That was the best one yet."

Lety had written Gunner's profile after Hunter had told her he was giving up on getting her back. In her heart, Lety knew she had to do something. She wrote the profile and gave it to Dr. Villalobos to share. He had been more than happy to send it to the Salazar family.

"Thank you, Lety," Hunter said with wet eyes. "It's true. You never give up."

James looked away from the profile toward Gunner and Hunter's little brothers.

"As soon as we read the profile, we knew what we had to do. Now that I see Gunner with you guys, I know we made the right decision."

"Thank you so much." Hunter beamed. He stood up quick and hugged James and the entire Salazar family. "This means so much to us, you don't even know."

"Thank you with all our hearts," Hunter's grandma said, rushing to embrace the family, too. Once all the hugs were over, Dr. Villalobos guided the Salazar family across the lawn to meet a few of the other shelter dogs.

Lety's family walked over to her with Spike on a blue leash. She still couldn't believe how amazing the day had turned out. Hunter slipped in next to her. "Can I meet your parents?"

"Okay, but they don't speak a lot of English." As they approached, Lety gestured toward Hunter, ready to make an introduction, but Hunter launched into Spanish!

"Señora y Señor Muñoz. *Mi nombre es* Hunter. *Yo soy un amigo de* Lety," Hunter said, introducing himself as Lety's friend. Lety giggled. "*Yo quiero dar gracias a ustedes porque* Lety *es muy simpática* — is that right, Lety?"

"Yes, I'm very nice," she said. Lety and Brisa laughed. Usually they were the ones pestering people if they said something right or wrong in English. It was fun to see Hunter making an attempt in Spanish.

"He's turning all red!" Eddie laughed and pointed at Hunter. Brisa quickly put her hands over Eddie's mouth, which made him laugh more.

"*Sin ella,*" Hunter continued. "*Nunca* . . . Sorry! I mean without her, my dog would never have been returned to me. I didn't practice this last part because I didn't know."

"I can translate," Eddie jumped in, and quickly rattled off Hunter's final words in Spanish to his parents. When he was done, they beamed with pride.

"You are welcome," Lety's mom and dad said together.

"We both have dogs, Hunter!" Lety said.

"Maybe we can go to the dog park together?" Hunter said. "What do you think? I think Spike and Gunner would get along." Before Lety could answer, he pointed across the lawn. "Check it out," he said. The two Salazar boys were petting Riley, the three-legged husky pup. "I think Riley is heading to Wichita."

Lety wondered if hearts could explode from so much joy as she watched Riley show off all his best tricks. He rolled over, picked up a stick with his mouth, and dropped it at James's feet. Riley sat up on three legs and tilted his head at them. Lety knew that adorable pose meant, "Don't you want to take me home?"

She hoped with all her heart that the kind Salazar family answered yes.

ChapTeR 29

Everyone Is Invited

The next day, the girls were at Kennedy's pool with Eddie and Spike. Hunter and Mario were each sprawled out on an inflatable doughnut in the pool, while Gunner took shade under a large umbrella.

"Are you guys coming to my birthday party?" Mario yelled to Lety and Brisa, who relaxed on lounge chairs. The girls had just received the invitation yesterday for Mario's pizza party.

"Are Gazi, Aziza, and Myra invited, too?" Brisa asked.

"I won't go if they're not invited also," Lety said.

"I invited everyone," Mario said. "Geesh! I even invited Kennedy, who hates my guts."

Lety and Brisa laughed and looked over at Kennedy, sunbathing on a lounge chair.

"I'm not here to hate," Kennedy said, pulling off her sunglasses. "I only celebrate."

"Alert! Alert! I think Spike wants to jump in," Hunter said. Lety scanned the pool area to find Spike pacing the edge of the pool like he was longing to swim.

"Don't you dare, Spike!" Kennedy yelled. "Lety, please stop him."

"C'mon, boy! Jump!" Eddie said from the water. "He wants to swim. Let him swim!"

"No dogs in the pool! No dogs in the pool!" Kennedy screamed just as Spike bounded into the pool. "Oh my! We're going to get kicked out." Kennedy sat up, watching with panic as Spike dog-paddled across the pool toward Eddie. Lety jumped up to grab him from the pool, but before she could, there was another blast of water.

"Gunner, no!" yelled Kennedy.

Gunner had dived in, too, splashing water in every direction.

"It's a pool pawty!" Mario yelled. "Get it?"

"Sorry, Kennedy!" Hunter apologized from the water.

"My mom is going to get a call from the HOA tonight," Kennedy said. "We'll be banned from the pool for the rest of the summer. I know it."

"Sorry, Kennedy," Lety said.

"I got them!" Hunter yelled, dog-paddling next to Spike and Gunner.

"*¡Lo siento,* Kennedy!*"* Eddie shouted from the pool.

"Hey, if you can't beat them, join them, right?" Lety said, taking Kennedy's hand and leading her to the edge of the pool. Lety grasped Brisa's hand, too.

"That's a silly expression," Kennedy said.

"At the count of three," Lety said. "Ready?"

"One!" Brisa shouted.

"Two!" Lety screamed.

"Three!" Kennedy squealed.

The three girls jumped into the pool, making a larger splash than Gunner.

When Lety came up for air, Gunner had a ball in her mouth and everyone was chasing her around the pool. Lety glanced around for Spike. He was already outside of the pool, dripping wet and waiting at the edge for her. She swam to him.

"Are you looking for me?" she asked. Spike let out an excited whine. "I love you and I'll never give up on you, Spike," she said before diving back down into the clear blue water. From above, she could hear Spike barking. She knew it was his way of saying, "I'll never give up on you, Lety."

acknowledgments

With love and gratitude to the following people:

My wonderful editor, Anna Bloom, for once again believing in my voice and the stories I want to tell.

The superb Scholastic team: Monica Palenzuela, Lizette Serrano, Emily Heddleson, and Robin Hoffman. Special thanks to Nina Goffi for creating beautiful book covers that capture the spirit of my stories.

Eternal gratitude to my agent at Full Circle Literary, Adriana Dominguez, for her continual guidance through this big scary publishing world and her unstoppable work to champion diverse kid lit and Latina authors like me. *¡Mil gracias*, Adriana!*

The Firehouse Five: Jane True, Victoria Dixon, Lisa Cindrich, and Shannon A. Thompson for not only sharing their wonderful manuscripts with me, but for providing supportive feedback during early revisions of this novel. A big hug to my young editor, Anna Walker, who provided me with generous encouragement.

Many people gave freely of their time and memories with

me so that I may capture the experience of an English Language Learner. Luisa Fernandez, whom I met in Kansas City, shared her stories as a young student from the Dominican Republic learning English in Missouri. Andrea Pardo-Spalding, a former ESL student in Kansas and now an architect. Both women shared many vivid and touching anecdotes that I used for this novel. Educators: Felicia Orozco, ESL teacher, and Carlota Holder, English Learner Coordinator, provided me with helpful insight into the ESL students' experiences in the classroom. Alejandra Subieta Jordan for always picking up the phone when I called and providing a voice for my beloved Brisa Quispe. *¡Muchas gracias, compañeras!*

While I was writing this book, there was one person who never seemed to tire of reading my drafts: my mom, a former fifth grade teacher. She'd come over to my house, sit out on the deck with a cup of *cafecito* and my fresh pages on her lap. Many times, in her typical teacher demeanor she'd pause her reading, put the manuscript down, and glance over at me to declare, "I've known a lot of Hunter Farmers in my career. That boy just needs someone to believe in him."

Thankfully, we have a world full of Hunters, Letys, and Brisas to keep us on our toes and hopeful for the future. With that, I want to give a big shout of love and encouragement to all the children learning English and Spanish or any new language. Don't let anyone silence you. Never stop dreaming big. Never give up!

Finally, I am grateful to my husband, Carlos Antequera, for his love, support, and patience throughout the writing of this novel.

Read the latest wish books!

Compelling stories of the heart from
ANGELA CERVANTES!

"Heartbreaking and
heartwarming."

—Diana López,
author of *Confetti Girl*

"Filled with gentle
humor, big lessons, and
even bigger heart."

—*Publishers Weekly*

⭐"Compelling and
relatable."

—*School Library Journal*,
starred review

scholastic.com

ACERVANTES2